D1518939

Nineteenth-Century American Musical Theater

General Editor
DEANE L. ROOT
University of Pittsburgh

A GARLAND SERIES

VOLUME 16

Grand Opera in America

The Scarlet Letter *(1896)*

MUSIC BY WALTER DAMROSCH, LIBRETTO BY GEORGE PARSONS LATHROP

Edited by
Elise K. Kirk
Catholic University of America

GARLAND PUBLISHING, INC.
NEW YORK AND LONDON 1994

Library of Congress Cataloging-in-Publication Data

Damrosch, Walter, 1862–1950.
[Scarlet letter. Vocal score]
Grand opera in America: The scarlet letter (1896) / music by Walter Damrosch; libretto by George Parsons Lathrop; edited by Elise K. Kirk.
1 vocal score.—(Nineteenth-century American musical theater; v. 16)
Reprint. Originally published: Leipzig: Breitkopf & Härtel, ca. 1906.
Includes reprint of the libretto originally published: Boston?: G.P. Parsons, 1895?, ca. 1894.
Includes bibliographical references.
ISBN 0-8153-1373-X
1. Operas—Vocal scores with piano. 2. Operas—Librettos. I. Lathrop, George Parsons, 1851–1898. II. Kirk, Elise K. (Elise Kuhl), 1932– . III. Hawthorne, Nathaniel, 1804–1864. Scarlet letter. IV. Damrosch, Walter, 1862–1950. Scarlet letter. Libretto. 1994. V. Title. VI. Title: Scarlet letter. VII. Series.
M1503.D166S3 1994 94–700554
CIP

Book design by Patti Hefner

Printed on acid-free, 250-year-life paper
Manufactured in the United States of America

Contents

Introduction to the Series

This series of sixteen volumes provides for the first time ever a comprehensive set of works from a full century of musical theater in the United States of America. Many of the volumes contain musical scores and librettos that have never before been published. Others make available works that were long lost, or widely scattered, or never before assembled in one place. Collectively, this series is the first substantial modern printing, not only of the individual titles it contains, but also of a repertory that is central to the nation's cultural history.

The prevailing view of nineteenth-century American theater is dominated by attention to the *words* voiced by the actors. But for most of this period theater simply did not operate from written texts alone; music was an equal and essential partner with the script. Music was so ubiquitous in the American theater throughout the nineteenth century that any understanding of the subject—or of individual works or theaters, indeed even of specific performances or performers—must take it into account. Yet few scholarly studies and still fewer modern editions of works have included the music as fully as the text. (An excellent summary of recent research, and of the problems created by lack of access to original complete works, is presented in Shapiro, 1987.)

Moreover, this series should help balance an emphasis in the scholarly literature on the bibliography of pre-1800 works at one end and the history and criticism of twentieth-century shows at the other, by providing a substantial body of material in between. Almost without exception, the works published here have been unavailable—even unknown except by reputation—to all but a handful of specialists. As Joseph Kerman has pointed out in his book challenging the field of musicology, research on musical theater is forty years behind most of the western music genres in that its "central texts" (the works themselves) have remained unavailable (Kerman, 1985, p. 48). In a sense, this series is a throwback to an earlier style of anthology delineated by geographical, chronological, and genre bounds, such as helped define historical national repertories for European scholars in the mid-twentieth century.

Until now, only a very few individual nineteenth-century musical-theater works have been issued in modern publications, sometimes—but not always—with the score alongside the libretto. Among the major scholarly series of editions that include musical-theater works performed in nineteenth-century America is A-R Editions' Recent Researches in American Music, which has made available William Shields's *The Poor Soldier* (1783), George F. Root's "operatic cantata" *The Haymakers* (1857), and Victor Pelissier's *Columbian Melodies* (1812) used in New York and Philadelphia theaters. A series from G.K. Hall, titled Three Centuries of American Music, has a single volume devoted to eighteenth- and nineteenth-century *American Opera and Music for the Stage* (1990), containing piano-vocal scores of Alexander Reinagle's *The Volunteers*, Rayner Taylor's *The Ethiop*, Arthur Clifton's *The Enterprise*, and Reginald de Koven's *Robin Hood.* And an English series of Music for London Entertainment 1660–1800, issued by Richard MacNutt (Tunbridge Wells) and later by Stainer & Bell (London), reproduces some works that were also performed in America.

Presented here by Garland Publishing, Inc., with full text and music, the forty-nine works in this series of sixteen volumes are now accessible not only to scholars of music, theater, literature, American studies, and other fields in the humanities and performing arts, but also to teachers and students in the classroom. Every work could be produced again on the stage, either as historic re-creation or in modern adaptation. The purpose of the undertaking is to make full works readily available for analysis, drama criticism, performance, and any other use by a modern academic audience as well as the general public.

The vast majority of surviving sources have lain scattered and hidden in public and private collections throughout the country, awaiting research that would piece them back together. At the time they were part of the living tradition of nineteenth-century American theater, such performance materials were considered functional and ephemeral. Their creators and users had little interest in preserving the works for posterity; they were much more mindful of the production at hand, of the business of attracting an audience and gaining its favor. If that meant keeping all the music scores in a trunk in a theater building prone to fire, or using scripts filled with up-to-the-minute changes, handwritten instructions, and typographical errors, or creating instrumental arrangements and musical insertions to the show without benefit of fully written-out scores, such were the necessities of life. Consequently they kept little, and published even less. (Sometimes their heirs, for whatever family interests they may have had, restricted access to the surviving sources for as much as a century. And even those materials that found their way into accessible archives have not been immune to loss by deterioration, misshelving, and pilferage.)

Most of the music that survives is in piano-vocal reduction from the theater-orchestra arrangements actually used. Much of it was printed and sold as souvenir selections for the musically literate public to use at leisure in their homes. Printed librettos were sold so that the audience could follow the performance at the theater.

This series strikes a balance between the more readily available printed piano-vocal selections and librettos, and the manuscript sources. In some cases, printed or manuscript musical excerpts have been reassembled to re-create a score the public never saw but which comes as close as possible to the melodies and harmonies that the theater musicians performed. In other volumes, the editors have drawn on contemporary sources to re-create the now-lost orchestration of the original theater arrangers (who would normally have been the resident conductors), or to assemble a full score from surviving orchestral parts. In only a few cases, original scores or librettos too indistinct or deteriorated to reproduce have been reset for clarity; we have sought to emphasize the value of seeing (reproducing) the *original* performance materials used in American theaters of the time. In every volume, the conditions of all known original sources and the circumstances surrounding their presentation in this series are clearly identified. Moreover, whenever possible the original sources are reproduced at actual size (although some have been altered slightly to fit the margins of modern printed books). Dates given in volume subtitles indicate the productions of the shows that generated the sources chosen to be reproduced.

The series aims to represent all the major genres and styles of musical theater of the century, from ballad opera through melodrama, plays with incidental music, parlor entertainments, pastiche, temperance shows, ethnic theater, minstrelsy, and operetta, to grand opera. These works reflect vividly the cultural mix of America: the incendiary *Uncle Tom's Cabin* stands alongside later shows written and performed by African-American troupes; the Irish and Yiddish theater in New York used language that modern audiences might not understand, but which was part of everyday life in the ghetto. At one end of the chronological spectrum we have shows imported by British immigrant musicians; at the other stands a grand opera written by the conductor of the Metropolitan Opera House, based on a great American novel.

The series General Editor has eschewed those titles, no matter how important, that are already available in full modern editions. Missing too are works, no matter how fine, of mostly local interest or regional significance. Nor is the series intended to suggest a core repertory, or a pantheon of masterworks. Rather, it is a selection of works by nineteen scholars active in research on a wide range of theatrical styles and cultural issues of the period.

Each volume of the series is complete in itself. Individual editors have each provided an introduction summarizing the careers and works of the composers and librettists. The introduction informs about the work(s) reproduced, giving dates and circumstances of first performances and any early revivals, origins of the plot and its treatment, and a brief critique explaining the historical importance of the work. The editors identify the locations of all significant original sources for each work, and any significant differences among them; they also note any other available performing materials that might be useful for a revival or detailed study (for example, a conducting score, other piano-vocal scores, instrumental parts, librettos, prompt books, stage designs, photographs, manuscript drafts). If the volume reproduces only a piano-reduction score, the editor's introduction identifies (as much as possible) the original instrumentation used in the theater. Recordings of any modern performances are mentioned, and a bibliography provides leads for further inquiry about the works and their creators. When necessary, notations have been made matching the musical selections of the score with their respective locations in the libretto.

Each volume editor has had principal responsibility for identifying the first or most appropriate copy available of the musical score and libretto. In selecting the copies to be reproduced, further preference has gone to those sources that are clean, untorn, and complete, which could be reprinted unedited. As is the nature of rare sources, the best exemplars are not always perfect ones, and we beg your patience with those that are less than ideal.

It is still true, as Anne Dhu Shapiro pointed out in 1987 (p. 570), that "the incomplete state of basic research in the area of musical theater . . . stands as the chief impediment to a better history." This series is offered with the hope and trust that it will foster greater understanding and contribute materially to the wider appreciation of America's heritage and traditions of musical theater.

Deane L. Root
University of Pittsburgh

Works Cited

Shapiro, Anne Dhu. Review of Julian Mates, *America's Musical Stage: Two Hundred Years of Musical Theatre*, in the *Journal of the American Musicological Society* XL/3 (Fall 1987): 565–74.

Kerman, Joseph. *Contemplating Music: Challenges to Musicology*. Cambridge, Mass.: Harvard University Press, 1985.

About this Volume

The most ambitious musical work for the American stage at the end of the nineteenth century was a grand opera, *The Scarlet Letter*, composed by Walter Damrosch, who as a conductor and impresario championed Richard Wagner's music in America. Anton Seidl, who conducted Wagner's first full Ring cycle in the United States, called *The Scarlet Letter* a "New England Nibelung Trilogy." The masterful and symbol-bound libretto is by George Parsons Lathrop, the son-in-law of Nathaniel Hawthorne, author of the classic novel on which the opera is based.

The success of this work—and its criteria for inclusion—cannot be measured in the same terms as for other titles in this series of *Nineteenth-Century American Musical Theater*. It did not receive hundreds or even dozens of performances, land even one melody in the nineteenth-century hit parade, or enter the repertories of touring companies. Nor did it help define the leading edge of a social or political movement, establish a new genre, or represent an emerging, oppressed ethnic minority.

Rather, *The Scarlet Letter* is something of a bridge, connecting strong constituencies within the musical, literary, and societal life of two centuries, but not itself achieving lasting prominence. Its composer, a German-born American citizen, represents the pinnacle of accomplishment and stature in turn-of-the-century classical-music circles; the librettist is old-line New England. The plot is provided by one of the most venerated and complex psychological American novels; its treatment as an opera libretto transforms it into an epic, sparer drama of ethics and morality. And, as historians and critics have noted, *The Scarlet Letter* pointed the way for more successful, fully American opera in the following century.

Damrosch was himself both a supporter of and a mediator between Germanophile and Americanist tendencies in music, between the monied institutions of high art and the accessible broadcast media that could reach virtually the entire population. Not unlike several other earlier composers of works in this series, he devoted significant portions of his career to conducting, to musical education, and to organizing his own performance company.

Fortunately, unlike so many other works in this series, *The Scarlet Letter* survives intact. Perhaps reflecting its origins among leading literary and musical personages of the era, a rather full set of performance materials exists, so that the editor did not have to reconstruct the work from disparate sources.

The editor of this volume, Elise K. Kirk, Ph.D., is co-editor of *Opera and Vivaldi* (University of Texas Press, 1984) and the author of *Musical Highlights from the White House* (Krieger, 1992). She teaches courses in American music at Catholic University of America, contributed extensively to *The New Grove Dictionary of Opera*, and is writing a history of opera in America.

D.L.R.

Introduction to this Volume

The Scarlet Letter (1896) by Walter Damrosch occupies a special place in the history and development of opera in the United States. It was the most ambitious grand opera of its era and the most significant since William Henry Fry's *Leonora* (1845). Janus-faced, it represents changing attitudes toward American musical theater as the century closed, while providing a springboard for a new line of American opera in the works of Parker, Converse, Herbert and others as the twentieth century began. *The Scarlet Letter* reflects an American society still under the thumb of European, especially Germanic, culture. But in the words of an early twentieth-century historian, it "shone serenely as the morning star of a new cycle in the history of this art" (Hipsher, p. 32).

Walter Damrosch (1862-1950), one of America's most renowned musical figures, was born in Breslau, Germany, and came to the United States at the age of nine. By the time he was twenty, he had conducted large orchestras and choruses in the works of Handel, Mendelssohn, Verdi, and Wagner. At the age of twenty-three, he succeeded his father, Leopold Damrosch, as conductor of both the Oratorio Society and the Symphony Society of New York (later the New York Philharmonic), holding the latter post for more than forty years.

Damrosch's lifelong love of opera was almost inevitable. His mother, the soprano Helene von Heimburg, had sung the role of Ortrud in the premiere of Wagner's *Lohengrin* at Weimar, and his father, a friend of Liszt and Wagner, organized the first productions of German opera at the Metropolitan Opera beginning with its second season, 1884–1885. From this period until 1891, Walter Damrosch served as assistant conductor, first under his father and later under Anton Seidl. These were the Wagner years, for during its early seasons, the Metropolitan presented the American premieres of *Die Meistersinger*, *Der Ring des Nibelungen*, and *Tristan und Isolde* and regularly produced many other Wagner operas. To spread further the music of the German master, Walter Damrosch founded his own touring opera troupe in 1894, the Damrosch Opera

Company. Until it was dissolved in 1900, this enterprising organization of nearly 200 members performed not only at the Metropolitan but introduced Wagner to principal cities as far west as Denver.

Walter Damrosch was also a distinguished music educator and champion of American music. He persuaded Andrew Carnegie to build Carnegie Hall, commissioned George Gershwin's Piano Concerto in F, and founded the American Conservatory at Fontainebleau, near Paris. During the early days of radio, Damrosch was one of the first to believe in its musical possibilities and through his numerous concerts and lectures brought music into millions of homes. Throughout his long life (he died at 88), Damrosch never abandoned his interests in opera, especially the German repertoire. And because his ultimate aim was to reach the public through music, he crusaded tirelessly for the production of foreign-language opera in English. In 1929 he was awarded the Bispham Memorial Medal of the American Opera Society, established to encourage the composition and performance of opera by American composers.

While Damrosch composed incidental music for Greek plays and a few pieces for piano and instrumental ensembles, his main interest lay in vocal genres. He wrote songs, choral works, compositions for solo voice with chorus and orchestra, and a stage piece he called an "operatic comedy" (*Elephants in Congress*, 1944). Damrosch composed five operas, which span his entire creative lifetime:

The Scarlet Letter in three acts; libretto by George Parsons Lathrop, after Nathaniel Hawthorne; portions performed in concert by Oratorio and Symphony Societies of New York, Carnegie Hall, January 4 and 5, 1895. Staged productions by the Damrosch Opera Company:
(1) Boston, Boston Theatre, February 10, 1896;
(2) Philadelphia, Academy of Music, February 22, 1896;
(3) New York, Academy of Music, March 6, 1896.

The Dove of Peace, comic opera in three acts; libretto by Wallace Irwin; Phildelphia, October 15, 1912.

Cyrano de Bergerac in four acts; libretto by William J. Henderson, after E. Rostand; Metropolitan Opera House, February 27, 1913; revised version in concert form, Carnegie Hall, February 20 and 21, 1941.

The Man without a Country in two acts; libretto by Arthur Guiterman, after Edward Everett Hale; Metropolitan Opera House, May 12, 1937, with soprano Helen Traubel in her Metropolitan debut.

The Opera Cloak, comic opera in one act; libretto by Gretchen Damrosch Finletter; New York, New Opera Company, Broadway Theater, November 3, 1942.

Throughout all of the operas, the influence of German Romanticism, especially Wagner, is paramount. *The Scarlet Letter* is so strongly fashioned after Wagnerian principles that it was called by Anton Seidl a "New England Nibelung Trilogy" (Damrosch, *Musical Life*, p. 116). *The Man without a Country* recalls the Singspiel, with its spoken dialogue and "astonishing freshness and infectious gusto," according to Lawrence Gilman (Hipsher, pp. 17–18). *Cyrano de Bergerac* is more eclectic, employing a Debussyan whole-tone scale motif to symbolize the protagonist's grotesque nose. Near the close of *The Opera Cloak* Damrosch experiments with a brief allusion to ragtime.

For his first major composition, Damrosch turned for inspiration to one of the greatest of the American novels, Nathaniel Hawthorne's brooding psychological romance, *The Scarlet Letter* (1850). It was a subject that had long fascinated the young composer, and he asked Hawthorne's son-in-law George Parsons Lathrop to prepare the libretto. Lathrop, the editor of Hawthorne's complete works published in 1883, was also a noted poet and author. His poetry for the opera libretto is often free, unrhymed and "molded by the sentiment, passion or situation of the moment," as he states in his introduction.

Lathrop's libretto is a masterful image of the novel. It retains the original setting in Colonial Massachusetts and most of the main events of the tragedy, although Pearl, Hester's child, is omitted in the opera. Lathrop, however, constructs the story around the primary thematic emphasis of the novel—sin and its effects on both the individual and society. Specifically, Hawthorne traces the effect of one particular sin on the lives of Hester Prynne, a woman convicted of adultery; Arthur Dimmesdale, the minister whose distressing secret ultimately kills him; and Chillingworth, Hester's malicious husband. Hawthorne, who anticipated Sigmund Freud's theories of the effects of guilt on the human spirit, was a skillful symbolist. Like the operas of Wagner, Hawthorne's novel abounds in symbols: the scarlet letter A that Hester must wear to display her sin, the scaffold of public notice, the sunlight in the forest, and the main characters themselves.

Thus it was not only the somber allegorical tale in its American setting that attracted Walter Damrosch, but also the story itself—a particularly striking parallel to that of the guilty lovers in *Tristan und Isolde*, produced nine years after Hawthorne's novel. Only the closing of the opera departs significantly from the novel: Hester takes poison and her "redemption" is realized as she dies with her lover. ("The flow of sacrifice / Blooms in no earthly garden / Thou, Hester, over us triumph hast won . . . .") While the opera compresses the novel's ending, it retains Hawthorne's ethical message through the townspeople, whose attitudes change dramatically from scorn and hatred to admiration and reverence.

Damrosch's score employs seven soloists, a large orchestra, and double choruses of four parts each. Wagnerian elements come to play in the harmonic language, orchestral fabric, and melodic techniques, which often utilize a leitmotif, such as the figure appearing in the orchestra whenever the scarlet letter is spoken of or suggested. Touches of dissonance and polytonal inflections underpin text or mood in prime moments of the opera, such as the chorale ("Praise God from whom all blessings flow") pitted against the agonized soloists in the closing scene of Act I.

While certain moments in the opera seem labored and lack musical and dramatic interest, others have a special beauty and charm, such as Hester's "Ripple of the Brook" at the opening of Act II, with its delicate text-painting in the harp and violins; her prayer of repentance with the organ coloring the instrumentation; and the madrigal-like chorus sung by the pilgrim immigrants from England that follows. Act III contains marked dramatic strokes in the "Shipmaster's Song" and the following scene between Chillingworth and Hester. As the critic in the *Boston Post* noted, "There is a masterly handling of the musical ideas and to those who find pleasure in the German School, 'The Scarlet Letter' will come as a welcome addition."

Reviews of the first performances were mixed, however. One noted critic, Henry Krehbiel, found the 34-year-old composer blending "the elements of his composition with a freedom and daring quite astonishing in their exhibition of mastery. There is no sign of doubt or timorousness anywhere in the work" (*Chapters*, p. 262). Another reviewer, Philip Hale, felt the opera lacked "dramatic vitality" and "melodic spontaneity." Still another compared the orchestra with a "tempestuous ocean in which a few musical phrases—chiefly Wagner's—float like débris after a shipwreck" (Remy, p. 574).

The work, nevertheless, was enthusiastically received by the audience, who thronged the theaters, stamping, applauding, cheering and demanding repeated curtain calls after each act. Flowers and huge laurel wreaths were bestowed on the composer of "the most ambitious American grand opera ever written" (*Boston Daily Globe*).

The cast for the premiere in Boston was essentially the same for the Philadelphia and New York productions:

Hester Prynne (soprano)	Johanna Gadski
Roger Chillingworth (baritone)	Wilhelm Mertens
Arthur Dimmesdale (tenor)	Barron Berthald
Rev. John Wilson (bass)	Gerhard Stehmann
Governor Bellingham (bass)	Conrad Behrens

Shipmaster (bass)	Otto Raberg
Brackett (bass)	Julius von Putlitz

An obvious weakness in the casting is the dominance of male roles, especially those in the lower registers. The singing of Johanna Gadski, however, drew repeated praise. The 23-year-old German soprano had recently made her American debut with the Damrosch Opera Company as Elsa in Wagner's *Lohengrin* and would become one of the finest Wagnerian singers in history. But Wilhelm Mertens proved a colorless Chillingworth. When the opera was produced in Philadelphia during the 1897–1898 season, Damrosch replaced him with the fine American baritone David Bispham, who was brilliant in this demanding role. "I reveled in the disagreeable but interesting character part of Chillingworth," said Bispham, "a part that I regret not having had any further opportunity to perform, as this interesting work has never, to my knowledge, been revived" (Bispham, p. 222). In the concert version of the opera performed in Carnegie Hall on January 4 and 5, 1895, the great Lillian Nordica sang the part of Hester and Giuseppe Campanari that of Chillingworth.

The staging of the opera was considered elaborate and well executed, but one hundred years too late for the seventeenth-century Boston of Hawthorne's story. Researched by the composer from early portraits, the costumes were termed "authentic," although they were criticized for being too colorful at times for the characteristic austere Puritan image. The choruses (often Handel-like in style) were described as animated and effective, adding a great deal to the overall staging and action (*Boston Daily Globe*).

Copies of the piano-vocal score and the libretto of *The Scarlet Letter* are in the Library of Congress and the New York Public Library at Lincoln Center (see the Bibliography). The full orchestral holograph remains unpublished and, with the copyist's manuscript of twenty-eight parts, is in the Music Research Division of the New York Public Library at Lincoln Center. The following instrumental parts are extant:

Violin 1, 2
Viola
Cello
Flute 1, 2, and 3 (piccolo)
Clarinet 1, 2, and bass clarinet
Oboe 1, 2
Bassoon 1, 2
Horns 1, 2, 3, 4
Trumpet 1, 2, 3
Trombone 1, 2, 3

Tuba
Timpani
Bass drum and cymbals
Harp

America had high hopes, indeed, for its "morning star" of grand opera. But for all the attention *The Scarlet Letter* attracted initially, critics and public alike did not consider it a true "American opera." Several decades later George Gershwin's *Porgy and Bess* provided some viable answers to a national dilemma, yet the search for an American operatic identity remains both timeless and timely. Like many American operas, those of Damrosch offer promises rather than solutions, and Krehbiel's words have a familiar ring: ". . . it [*Cyrano de Bergerac*] will encourage native composers to work, and through their strivings there may yet be found a style of operatic writing adapted to the genius of our language and appealing to the taste of the American people" (in Broekhoven, p. 1125).

Sources

Libretto and vocal score courtesy of the Library of Congress, Washington, D.C.

Bibliography

Published Sources

"American Grand Opera—First Performance Here of Walter Damrosch's 'Scarlet Letter.'" *New York Times* (March 7, 1896).

Bispham, David. *A Quaker Singer's Recollections*. New York: Macmillan, 1921.

"Boston's Own Opera—Splendid Success of Damrosch's 'The Scarlet Letter.'" *Boston Daily Globe* (February 11, 1896).

Broekhoven, J. Van. "*Cyrano*—Walter Damrosch's New Opera as Produced at the Metropolitan Opera House, February 27: A Descriptive and Thematic Analysis." *The Musical Observer* (March, 1913): 1121–1126.

Damrosch, Walter. *My Musical Life*. New York: C. Scribner's Sons, 1923. Reprint Westport, Conn.: Greenwood Press, 1972.

_____. *The Scarlet Letter*, Op.1. Opera in three acts. Words by George Parsons Lathrop after Hawthorne's romance. Vocal score by the composer. Leipzig and New York: Breitkopf & Härtel, 1896.

Hale, Philip. "Scarlet Letter and Grand Opera." *Boston Journal* (February 11, 1896).
Hipsher, Edward Ellsworth. *American Opera and Its Composers*. Philadephia: Theodore Presser Co., 1934. Reprint New York: Da Capo Press, 1978.
Howard, Polly Damrosch, and Anita Damrosch Littell. "Walter Damrosch and Opera," *Opera News* (January 27, 1962): 8–13.
Krehbiel, Henry Edward. *Chapters of Opera*. New York: Henry Holt & Co., 1909. Reprint New York: Da Capo Press, 1980.
_____. "The Scarlet Letter." *Musical Courier* 30, no. 2 (1895): 13–15.
Lathrop, George Parsons. *The Scarlet Letter*, dramatic poem for the opera by Walter Damrosch. Libretto with "Introductory Note" by the author, January, 1895. Boston: George Parsons Lathrop, 1894 [*sic*].
Martin, George. *The Damrosch Dynasty: America's First Family of Music*. Boston, Houghton Mifflin, 1983.
_____. "Mr. Walter Damrosch's Opera—Extracts from the 'Scarlet Letter' at a Symphony Concert." *New York Times* (January 6, 1895).
Remy, Alfred. "The Scarlet Letter," *The Looker-On* (April 1896): 569–76.
"The Scarlet Letter: First Performance on Any Stage," *Boston Post* (February 11, 1896).

Unpublished Sources

Damrosch Family Collection, Music Division, Library of Congress. Includes programs, clippings, photographs, scrapbooks, and scores from the career of Walter Damrosch.
Walter Damrosch Collection, Special Collections, Music Research Division, New York Public Library at Lincoln Center. Primarily correspondence, iconography and music manuscripts, including the holograph full orchestral score and orchestral parts for *The Scarlet Letter*.

E.K.K.

Index of Musical Numbers

Title | *Score Page*

Act III

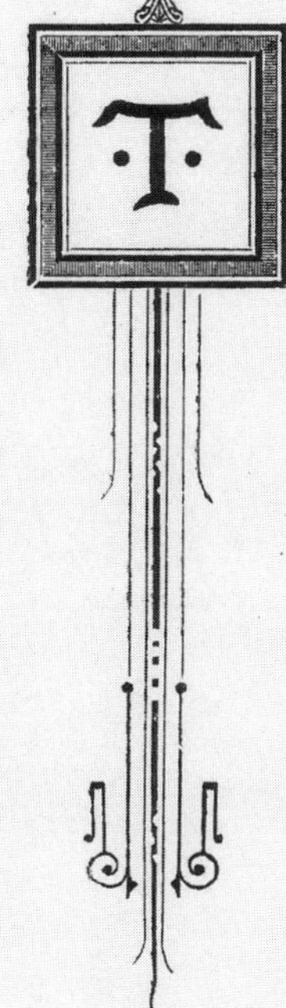

The Scarlet Letter . . .

DRAMATIC POEM

- BY -

GEORGE PARSONS LATHROP

OPERA BY WALTER DAMROSCH

THE

SCARLET LETTER

DRAMATIC POEM

· · BY · ·

GEORGE PARSONS LATHROP

MUSIC BY

WALTER DAMROSCH

Persons Represented.

ARTHUR, - - - - - - —

HESTER, - - - - - - —

CHILLINGWORTH, - - - - - —

WILSON, - - - - - - —

BELLINGHAM, - - - - - —

BRACKETT, - - - - - - —

A SHIPMASTER, - - - - - —

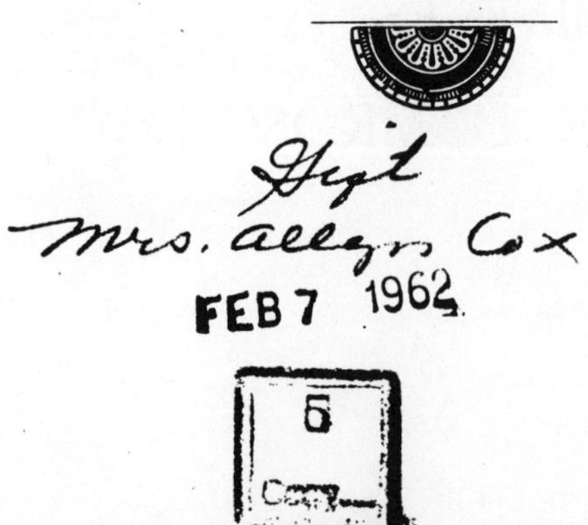

Introductory Note.

When Mr. Walter Damrosch asked me to write a Dramatic Poem suited for the music of a Grand Opera, on the theme of Hawthorne's "Scarlet Letter," two important artistic requirements had to be taken into view: First, it was necessary to make the movement of the piece quick and eminently dramatic. Secondly, the lines must be not only *singable* in rhythm and in succession of vowel sounds, but must have a quality that would promote or coöperate with a rich and impassioned musical expression.

It is but fair to say that the dramatic construction was the result of collaboration by the composer and the author, and was largely suggested by Mr. Damrosch. Obviously the character of Little Pearl was impossible in opera, and she was therefore omitted. The great elemental story of Hester's and Arthur's love, sin, suffering and partial expiation is what we wished to treat. This is presented with the utmost directness and compression. Gaps are bridged, delays avoided. Incidents are changed, remodelled or transposed at will, and new incidents and moods are introduced.

No attempt has been made to reproduce or to follow exactly the great prose romance from which the story is drawn. I do not suppose, either, that I have adapted from Hawthorne's pages more than two dozen sentences, if so many, in the whole work. My text is an original Dramatic Poem on the old theme.

It stands, therefore, as a new work, which may be read for itself. But it is also designed, in every line, for music and song. I used an entire freedom in the form and the varying measures employed. To write verse suited to musical conceptions, and to interpretation by the orchestra and voice, however, is almost a distinctive branch of the poetic art. The poem must have abrupt changes of time and character, not always conforming to the traditions of verse meant only for reading, but obeying a large artistic law. In this poem of

"The Scarlet Letter" a greater variety of feet, measures and stanzas is brought into play. The form was moulded by the sentiment, passion or situation at each moment.

Besides the metre and rhythm of each line, regarded separately, there is often a complicated word melody, or a scheme of emphases and pauses, running through several lines. These three, as a simple instance, while having each its own "time," belong to one continuous rhythm, and must be taken together to complete it :

> " For thee I would rule
> By thy shattered heart
> And truth forsworn."

Such "over-rhythms," as they might be called, correspond frequently to continuing strains in the music. It will be seen, then, that rhyme is in many places not essential. Although I have used it freely, I drop it the instant it might interfere with finer effects. In other places, where there may be an appearance of partial rhyme, rhyme has not been sought for, but only that kinship of vowel-sounds called assonance. It may be well to add that certain faltering effects, or irregularities, are intentional, where regularity or smooth and rounded verse forms would have failed to convey the mood or emotion needing to be expressed.

GEORGE PARSONS LATHROP.

January, 1895.

THE SCARLET LETTER.

ACT I.

The Market-Place, Boston, with Prison at L., a rosebush in bloom growing by the door. At back, a Church or Meeting-House. At R., the Town Hall, and near it the Pillory, R. C. Openings on either side of the Meeting-House, giving a view of Boston Harbor.

Puritan men and women, entering through these streets and at sides, assemble in excitement.

MASTER BRACKETT, *the Jailer, with a company of Soldiers, stands near the Prison door.*

CHORUS OF PURITAN MEN AND WOMEN.

Chorus. How boldly shines the sun!
Yet outer darkness
Enfolds yon wicked woman: while, within her,
The wrong that she hath done
Gleams bold as bale-fire 'gainst the light of day.
O child of error, fair,
Caught in her beauty's own unhallowed snare;—
How boldly shines the sun
To flare upon her shame!
But she, with soul that burns in angry flame,
Stays close in her prison.
There, there she lurks—the sinner,
Hiding herself away.
Quick! Bring her forth.

Brackett. Who dares here command ?
The Governor cometh :
He only hath power to condemn.
Wait justice, then, at his hand.

[*Pushing aside the people.*

Aside, there, stand ;—
Asidê, I say !
You bluster like the wind,
For your will is the wind's rough way.

Chorus. The woman hath foully sinned,
Yet vengeance slumbers.
To our folk she must expiate
The shame she hath bro't on them.

[*They surge towards the jail as if to attack it.*

Brackett. Be silent. Hearken !

Chorus. Hester, the sinner !
Bring forth the offender.
If she stood here before us,
For pity or pardon
To sue and implore us.
No mercy would lighten her burden ;
For judgment stern we would render.
To crime give its guerdon :
Her sin is abhorrent :—
Death's doom we would award her,
Since the law gives us warrant.
To judgment ! Condemn her !

[*They make another rush at the jail, but are beaten back by the soldiers.*

Brackett (*to the soldiers*). Guard the gate !

Enter CHILLINGWORTH, *unobserved.*

Chill. What wrathful sound is this that rises loud ?
How fierce their anger 'gainst an erring woman !
O strange ! Tho' oft I've heard the hungry storm
Roar for its prey ;—sharp winds of ocean moaning ;—
More dreadful is this cry of human hearts
That know not mercy.

Brackett. Behold, she comes !

Chorus. She comes!

[*The prison door opens. Crowd subsides into momentary hush. In the dark shadow of the corridor within the prison door a red glow is seen proceeding from a lantern hanging there. The soldiers form a lane through the crowd from the prison door to the pillory.*

Chorus. Hush, hush! Behold
From the prison gleams
A glowing flame.
See you not? See you not?

[*Enter from prison door a jailer, followed after a brief pause by* HESTER. *She stands for a moment on the door-step, silent, dignified, yet woe-begone.* HESTER, *accompanied by* BRACKETT, *crosses stage towards the Pillory. Some of the crowd point at the Scarlet Letter on her breast. Others turn away or shield their eyes as though horror-stricken and blinded by it.*

[CHILLINGWORTH, *roused by their cries, moves to where he can see Hester, and gazes at her, at first curiously.*

Chill. This creature—who?
Nay, what horror! 'Tis Hester—
My wife! My wife!

Chorus. Jezebel! Jezebel!
Daughter of hell!
See how serpent-like it twines,
Yon letter, with its coiling lines;
As though it were clutching her breast,
Of her soul in quest.
Lo, she sports with her shame,
And hath woven the letter
With gaudy splendor of scarlet.
The token that should be her fetter
She turns to a mocking flame
Of adornment. Down with the cursèd harlot!
Punish her evil doing;—
Banish her shadow, that darkens
Each true Puritan dwelling,
Staining us all with dishonor;

Tempting God's wrath, in disaster.
Far into hell-fire cast her.
Down with the cursèd harlot!

[BRACKETT *and the Soldiers protect* HESTER *from crowd. Reaching Pillory, she ascends it, and stands alone there, defiant.*

Chill. O blasting mockery! O bleak despair!
All mercy withers now in fires of hate;
And from my heart, like a black smoke, rolls up
Revenge!

[*Drum roll heard.*

[*Enter, on the balcony of the Town Hall,* ARTHUR DIMMESDALE, *with his senior colleague,* REV. JOHN WILSON; GOV. BELLINGHAM *and other dignitaries, attended by four sergeants.*

Wilson. Hester Prynne, hearken!
Thy husband absent,
Far beyond sea—
A child to thee here was born,
Bringing disgrace and scorn.
Heaven's wise decree
Hath taken thy daughter away,
Wafted on wings of death.
If with her thou wouldst feel
Heaven's holy breath,—
No longer thy secret conceal,
But thy fellow-offender accuse.

[*Pause.*

Hast thou no word to say?

[*Hester remains silent.*

Dost thou refuse?

[*Hester is still silent.*

[*To* HESTER, *laying his hand on* ARTHUR'S *shoulder.*

With my brother I've striven,
My colleague pastor—
This godly youth;—
That here in the face of heaven
He deal with you, touching the truth:
That no longer you hide
His name who wrought you this wrong
And led to your grievous falling.
Guilt-burdened, bow your pride
Of sin: Hear conscience calling!

Bellingham (*to* ARTHUR).

Yea, worthy sir.
You are her pastor and preacher.
Speak with her; plead—.
Exhort her; beseech her.

(*To* HESTER.)

Tho' thou hast wandered,
Far from the true path straying;—
The evil is in the deed,
Not in the saying.
Therefore take heed:
Confess! Confess!
And the powers of heaven may bless
Your late relenting.

(*To* ARTHUR.)

But you, O gentle brother,
Alone can prove
If she have grace for repenting;
This hapless mother,—
Lost wife beguiled
By alien love,—
Whom fate holds far from her husband,
And death despoils of her child.

Chorus. Yea, worthy one, deal with this woman's soul.

Arthur. Thou hearest them, Hester Prynne,
And, alas, thou seest
The maze of grief wherein
I walk, the least
Of those who dare sinners upbraid.
Thy welfare was in my keeping;
And so thy sin must be mine.
Fully *thou* hadst faith in thy guide:
All the more, therefore,
Imploring—yea, weeping—
My prayer must ascend for pardon.
Why, then, dost thou make no sign?
Nay, think; if thy lips thou harden,
Then I,—for thy poor soul's sake
That I so care for,
And even death would dare for—
Thy burden of silence upon me take.

Chorus. O wise and child-like,
Simple and pure ;—
With words of an angel he speaks !

Arthur (*to* HESTER).
Not so ; but of one who seeks
To save thee from dole.
If peace to thee it would give,
And thy spirit make whole,
Or hope of salvation insure,—
Tell his name who with thee now suffers,
Though hiding his guilty heart.
High or low, spare him not from the ban.
Be not too tender,
Nor pity render
To him who, so, may be tempted
To play the dissembler's part.
Remember, he is not exempted
From the doom that shadows thee.
Think, ere thou repliest ;
For if the truth thou deniest,
O Hester, Hester !—
His soul with thine condemned may be.

[ARTHUR *sinks back, exhausted, with hand over heart.* BELLINGHAM *and* WILSON, *anxious, support him.*

Chorus. Look, look ! He reels
And trembles. Too sharp the stress
Of grief that he feels
For the wanton's woe.
Though fallen low,
Base woman, thou shouldst be proud
Of the wretchedness
His pity deigns to bless.
Answer him, aloud.

Arthur (*rousing himself to fresh effort*).
Ay. Tell them who tempted thee.

Hester (*gently*). From me the world shall never know his name.

Wilson. Confession and repentance may avail
To take the scarlet letter off thy breast.

Hester (*looking at* ARTHUR).
It is too deeply branded.
Ye cannot take it off !

Arthur. Speak out the name :

Chorus. Speak, speak !

Chill. (*from crowd*). Ay, woman ; speak,
And give thy child a father !

Hester (*startled and agitated*). Ha ; that voice—
No, no ; thrice no, to thee ! My child hath found
A heavenly father. Ye shall never know
Its earthly one.

ENSEMBLE.

ARTHUR, CHILLINGWORTH, BELLINGHAM, WILSON, HESTER, CHORUS.

Arthur.
O marvel ! She will not speak.
O wondrous kindness of a woman's heart !
Reproach to my soul,
And agony deep !
For while I keep
My secret apart,
She, alas, undefended,
This open scorn
Alone must endure.
Maddening silence,
Torture accurst,
That burns the soul
Like lips athirst
Where hell-fires roll :
Ah, would the torture were ended !
Yet, ah, though humbly
I here were to kneel,
My guilt to unfold,—
Fair fame and falsehood spurning—
Too late for her weal
The truth would be told :
For the flowering dawn
Of her womanhood pure
Is lost in the hot noon's burning.

Chill.
Then, if she will not speak,
Hell close her lips, but open her heart to me
He who has betrayed
My sacred trust,

To me shall atone.
Ay ; vengeance is just,
And in vain all concealing.
The traitor unknown
At my feet shall be laid,
Himself to me revealing.
But thou, who hast broken
Thy vow in disgrace,—
May the governor spare thee !
For thee I would rule
By thy shattered heart
And truth forsworn.
Till I ensnare thee,
And make thee mourn
Thine evil part,
And his, poor fool,—
With double woe contending.

Chorus. She will not speak :
O devil-bound spirit !
What ! here among us
Shall we then cherish
Satan's own seed ?
Nay, from the land let her perish !
Ay; give her death !
Worshipful governor,
Dally not long
With her stubborn wrong,
Who shows no repentance ;
But swift unto death
Give thou her sentence !
To death !
Hearken, all hearken !
What may he declare,—
Our ruler undaunted ?
The doom in his face
By compassion is haunted :
Would he grant her a grace,
And will he so dare ?
Nay, then, we demand
That the woman, banned
By law, shall have death,—
The wage of her dark offending !

Wilson.

She will not speak :
'Tis death within her soul that makes her dumb.
Yet not in vain
May pity seek
To wake again
The soul from trance,
Its slumber imbuing
With eager breath.
Let mercy be ours,—
Her life renewing.
O powers of heaven,
Give judgment wise
To thy servants here,—
That we to this woman
Your will may truly make known !
Let your light on us rise,
And your glory appear
In the words of the just ;—
Or be it with death or life she atone.

Hester.

Maddening silence,
Torture accurst,
That burns the soul
Like lips athirst
Where hell-fires roll !
Almighty Father,
End thou this woe !
Whatever doom to me shall come,
Spare not my sin ;
But lay me low,
Despised, accurst ;
And save him, first,—
That he may win
The boon of thy pardon descending !
To guard his honor
He, too, must be dumb ;
But alas for the grief
In his bosom pent as a prison !
May mercy, like rain
On the withering leaf,
His spirit renew,
Till his life upspring,
As a flower when dawn has arisen.

Bellingham. Tho' we slay her, still lives the father
We vainly have sought.
Young, fair, of her husband forsaken,—
So was her honor shaken,
Her ruin wrought.
Defiant, unbending,
She will not speak?
Yet loth am I to array,
The law's last power to say,
Her life shall now have ending.
I dare not condemn her!
For may it not be
That slow, sad time
And penance profound
Her heart will subdue?—
Till the truth of her prime
She seek to renew?
Hear, then! I decree
Not death. She is free——

(*End of Ensemble.*)

Chorus. She is free!

Bellingham. But henceforth apart
From other folk she must tarry;
And there on her heart,
Her life long, carry
Yon Scarlet Letter!

[HESTER *clutches at her bosom convulsively, and bows her head.*

Chorus (*mocking her*). The scarlet woman
And Scarlet Letter!
What retribution better!
Ha, ha! Ha, ha!
All her life hereafter
Round her shall ring scorn and laughter.

Bellingham (*to* WILSON). Now, worthy minister,
For prayer and sermon!
Pour on the multitude
The dew of Hermon—
Thy balmy eloquence;—
That in union we dwell together.

[*To the crowd.*

Into the church,
Good people, repair.

[WILSON *and the others enter the Meeting House. As* ARTHUR *passes the Pillory his glance meets* HESTER'S. *He turns away with bowed head, his hand clutching his breast, and hurriedly enters the Meeting House.* HESTER *remains standing on the Pillory, and* CHILLINGWORTH *lingers near her.*

Hester. My heart is broken.
O shame and sorrow!
How shall I face the morrow,—
Wearing this token?

[*Sinks down, fainting.*

Chill. (*rushing up Pillory steps*).
What has chanced here?
She must not die.
Now, necromancy,
Come to my aid!

[*He mixes a potion in a leathern cup, which, with case bottles, he takes from his girdle; and pours the draught within her lips.*

Hester (*partly recovering*).
To mine anguish leave me:—
I am not afraid
To perish alone!

Chill. Nay, look. It is I.
Dost thou not know me?

Hester (*starting up*). Thou! Thou?—
Roger Prynne, of the darkling brow!
Whence comest thou here?

Chill. Hush, Hester. Have no fear.

Hester (*trying to conceal the Scarlet Letter*).
But if thou know'st—

Chill. The worst I know!

[*A pause.*

Far over ocean straying
Thee still—tho' long delaying—
I came to find.
But, lo, the unfaithful sea,
Wrecking us, cast me ashore

On a wild coast:
Whence, wandering long,
Through the silent forest,
Thee still to find, I came;—
Till here in the market-place
I beheld thy face
And thine open shame—
My wife!

Hester, (*in agony growing faint again*).
Oh! I can bear no more!
[*She droops, and is supported by* CHILL.

CHORAL.

(*Heard within the church.*)

Praise God, from whom all blessings flow;
Praise Him, all creatures here below!
Praise Him above, ye heavenly host,
Praise Father, Son, and Holy Ghost.

Chill. (*proffering cup anew*).
Drink this. Be strong.

Hester. Will it bring me death?
Then gladly I drink it,
To win release.
[CHILL. *presses the cup upon her, and she drains it.*

Chill. (*after she has drunk*).
No; it gives thee life,
And keeps thee living,
That so thine infamy's mark
Still may burn on thy bosom.

Hester. O pitiless, thou! and strange
The charm thy potion has wrought;
As though all my thought
Were artfully lulled, by thy soothing,
To some dark spell.

Chill. Yea;—never to tell
Thy secret, save to me.
I ask not wherefore
Nor how you fell.

Since, from my birth deformed—
The fault was mine
To dream you loved me.

(*Choral ends.*)

Hester. Love I felt not, nor feigned.

Chill. Yet thou hast wronged me,
And the man still is living
Who wronged us both.
For him there can be no forgiving.
Speak, Hester. Who is he?

Hester. Nay, ask me not! No power
Can wring from me his name.

Chill. As in books I've sought truth,
Or, in alchemy, gold;
Him I'll hunt without ruth
Till his secret I hold.

Hester (*shuddering*). And then—you would kill?

Chill. Nay. Let the man live!
I obey heaven's will.

Hester. If its mercy should give
That in honor he bide?

Chill. Like a star let him shine!
Yet, wherever he hide,
He is mine! He is mine!

Hester. Thy deeds feign mercy,—but thy words are terror.

Chill. Thou'st kept the mystery of thy paramour;
One thing I ask: that thou keep, also, mine.
None know me in this land; yet here's my home,
Near thee—near him. But thou—betray me not!

Hester. Why dost thou lay upon me this command?

Chill. Thy husband, to the world, is as one dead:
Henceforth the name of "Chillingworth" I wear.
Thou, recognize me not by word or sign,
Nor breathe our secret to the man thou knowest;
For if thou dost, his fame, his life will be
Mine to destroy. Hester, beware! beware!

Hester. I will be secret, then, for thee—for him.

Chill. (*smiles grimly*).
Ay; dwell in darkness, ever.

Hester. How strange thy smile!
Oh! art thou like the Black Man of the forest?
Hast thou enticed my soul into a bond
Of ruin?

Chill. Thy soul, Hester? No; not thine!

(*Choral begins again within Church.*)

"God's voice breaks cedars; yea, God breaks cedars of Lebanus."

[*Tumult and cries heard within church. The people troop forth in confusion, excited, with* BELLINGHAM, *etc. Some of them carry* ARTHUR *in their arms.*

Chorus. He has fainted. Air!
Help, help for our saintly pastor!

Hester. Arthur! Arthur!
How ghostly pale!

[*She runs to him swiftly; drops on her knees by him, anxious. The crowd angrily drive her away.*

Chorus. Back, woman! Thy touch
To his white soul is pollution.

Chill. 'Tis he. O wonder of darkness,—
I have found the man!

[CURTAIN.]

ACT II.

The Forest. HESTER'S *Hut, on one side. At back an opening among the trees, showing a forest path lost in obscurity. Sunlight alternates with deep shadow. Indications of a brook among the trees; the light sparkling on it fitfully.*

Enter HESTER *from the Hut.*

Hester.

Ripple of the brook, and rest of the sunshine
Asleep under trees :—
Restless am I as the water's murmur
And wandering breeze.
Sunlight flies from me ere I near it :—
The brook's moan stays !
Grief never dies from me ; still I hear it,
Through nights and days,
Sob 'mid the woodland—the stream intoning
My heart's own woe.
Ah, sad brooklet, why still art moaning ?
What dost thou know ?
Is it a secret of this dark forest
Told unto thee ;—
Fearsomely wrong, that thou abhorrest,
And so must flee,
Whispering ever the hapless tidings ?
Couldst thou but cease ;—
Hushing thy plaint, with my spirit's chidings ;—
I should find peace !

[HESTER *sinks down upon a mossy bank by the brook, musing. A pause, the music continuing.*

Hester.

Ah, still how gently,
Blending, returning,
With long endeavor—
Fleeting as foam,

Yet enduring forever—
Sweet thoughts of home
Awake in me yearning!
And still my heart doth wander
Far to its childhood blest
In England yonder.
O, innocence! flown like a bird from the storm-blown nest—
Come back to me!
Dreams of the church-bell, and prayers that I knew—
Come true, come true!

[*She kneels.*

O Father in heaven! if still
To call thee Father I dare:—
Grant me to do thy will;
My burden here to bear!
Unto my heart restore
Sweet faith again, and rest,
That humbly I once more
May trust my soul to thy care.

[*After a pause there is heard in the distance a madrigal sung by new Pilgrims, from England, who gradually draw nearer.*

MADRIGAL (*of the new Pilgrims*).

Green are the meads
Made new by showers,
And hedgerows white
With hawthorn flowers
Win our hearts to delight.
Who'd then at home be staying?
Up; cast aside dull sorrow's weeds:
'Tis time we go a-Maying.

To the daisy's breast
The larks, above us,
Rain down heaven's song:—
"Oh listen, and love us!"
And all the day long
Among the daisies playing,
We remember their strain, a dream of the blest!
For so we go a-Maying.

Hester. Hark! How those voices
Make answer to my longing
With song well known to me of yore,
That now, returning, my spirit rejoices,
And brings dear memories thronging
Back from the days of old !

Enter a band of Pilgrims, with women, children, etc.

[HESTER *advances, hesitating, towards the group, as though to welcome them.*

Two Puritan Men (*accompanying the Pilgrims as guides*).
Nay ; hold her aloof.
A witch she is,
And wanton, too ;—
An outcast soul.
Beware !

[*The Pilgrims draw away from* HESTER *in dread and scorn.* HESTER, *suddenly remembering, shrinks, clutching the Scarlet Letter. The others continue to move away.*

Hester (*alone*). O Ruler of heaven !
Are these thy creatures ?
Can it be, Thou hast given
To men thy features—
With hearts of clay
And lips of flame,
To blacken thine image
And a soul to blast in Thy name ?
Ah, then farewell
To meek repentance :
No longer I dwell
In mercy's bound.
Lord, give them sentence
Of anguish profound !—
As I, too, fling them my curse,
Like a brand from the fire of my bosom.
May it burn and wither
Their wandering souls,
Hither and thither ;—
Cling to them, haunting,
And humble their vaunting.

To crumble in ashes
Of endless death!

[*Goes into her hut, with a gesture of despair.*

The scene darkens, as though with a passing Cloud.

Enter CHILLINGWORTH *and* GOVERNOR BELLINGHAM.

Bellingham. What cry was that?

Chill. The wildwood, sighing.

Bell. Nay, rather the wail
Of human sorrow undying.

Chill. Portents prevail
In this favored land,
Where only a barrier frail
Between spirit and flesh may stand.
Belike you heard
Some evil bird,
Or the shriek of a dark soul winging
Its way to the nether world.

Bell. Most learned leech,
Thou art so skilled
In nature-speech,
With marvel filled,—
Tell me, canst thou yet reach
The source of wasting woe
That, with agony slow,
Consumes the life
Of Arthur, our friend?

Chill. A strife without end!
The ancient mystery
Of body and mind.
Hidden and strange the history!

Bell. Much do I fear,—
So great his worth,
So tender his spirit and pure,—
Not long he will endure
These bonds of earth,
But, leaving us lonely,
Take flight to heaven.

Chill. To heaven? No, no!
Of such disaster be sure
There need be no dread.
I would not grieve thee,—
With thoughts of woe.
Arthur I guard, as the night guards a flower
From the sun strong-rayed.
If the blossom shall flourish
Or fail and fade,—
Not well may I know.

Bell. Thou knowest him dear to us:
Save him; oh, save!
Hold him still near to us,
Far from the grave.

Chill. Deep within me I nourish
Desire that he live.
And ere he should perish,
My soul to perdition I'd give.

Bell. Thou lovest him well.

[*Exit Bellingham.*

Chill. (*alone*). Ay, indeed—with the love of hell!
With such love here I await
The holy man.
Why does he linger afar, so late?
To yonder lonely mission he fared
Of Eliot, our Indian apostle.
Ha! can it be he has fancied or dared
My grasp to elude?
In vain were the plan!
For his life is pursued
By the silent foot-fall, still, of my hate.
Round him is woven the web of his fate,
While I, ever near,
As leech and friend,
Have watched the quivering wounds of his soul.
My skill alone has kept him whole;
That over him, so, I might gloat, to the end.
No, no; he shall not die!
As music his cries of pain
Ring sweet through my brain;
And I live by my joy in his agony.
He shall have life,—

Long life of restless days,
And nights of endless woe!

Enter, from the forest, ARTHUR.

Arthur (*startled*). What! Is it thou—
My kind physician?
Chill. Yea, Arthur; waiting;
For even now
Methought thou wouldst return.
Arthur. Good friend, I feel
Thy kindly will;
Yet sometimes, weary, the soul
Must wander still,
With only God for its goal.
Chill. Yet in thy weakness
'Tis best thou lean on me,
And yield with meekness;
For a grief at the spirit's core,
Like smouldering flame,
Will set its mark
On the outward frame.
Wouldst have me heal
Thy bodily woe?—
Lay open the dark,
Deep trouble or wound in the soul below.
Arthur. No, no;—to thee? No;
Nor to any physician of earth!
For a soul's disease
To the healer of souls
I go; since He, as Him it may please,
Can kill or can cure.
But who art thou,
With daring so sure
Thyself to thrust
'Twixt the sufferer's dearth
And the bounty supreme, all-wise, of his God?
Chill. Nay; I but told you
That which I must.
Be patient; and heed;
Thy strength guard well.
Election sermon to-morrow thou preachest.

Thy mind must be calm,
To weigh what thou teachest,
And minister balm
To thy reverent flock
Who bow before thee
And truly adore thee—
Their shepherd, their saint and sheltering rock.
Too well thy tender pity I know.
Thy heart still bleeds for another's woe,
And is ever oppressed
With the sorrow of her whose wrong is confessed.

Arthur. Ha! Thou meanest——

Chill. Hester Prynne!

[ARTHUR, *greatly agitated, seems about to remonstrate, or deny; but* CHILLINGWORTH *continues.*

Nay; dare not protest:
Thou shalt not deny!
Turmoil of soul above all must thou dread;
For it saps thy force, and deepens disease.
So good I know thee, so saintly kind,—
For this poor woman thou long hast repined.
And so have I!
But now, instead,
Calm thy compassion! Canst not appease
Her conscience with thy sympathy?

[*Indicating* HESTER'S *hut.*

Lo, here she dwells:
And, now we are nigh,
Wilt thou not see her?

Arthur (*excited, amazed*).
I?—Thou forgetest—
How may it be,
Since here, condemned, she dwells apart?

Chill. Thou art her pastor. Thou hast the right
To see her, talk with her—heart to heart.

Arthur. Dost thou think that *I*, then——

Chill. Yea; thou of all men:
Thy heart is so pure.
Ah, go to her. Go!

Arthur. And thou!—Dost thou wait near?

Chill. Nay ; homeward I fare :
These herbs I now must distill.

Arthur (*gives token of relief ; aside*).
At last ! At last !

Chill (*aside*).
Now let her deal with the man as she will,
And the black flower blossom as it may !

Arthur (*to* CHILL.).
For a time, farewell.

Chill. I go. (*Aside.*) Fare ill !

[*Exit* CHILLINGWORTH.

Arthur (*alone*). So long it seems—long years !—
I have dwelt amid darkness and tears,
In the bonds of sin :
While evil has gnawed at my life, without,
And remorse has drained it, within.
And long, ah, long since I knew
The touch of a happiness true,
Or words without fear !
Would God I might break the chains of doubt,
And call to thee, Hester ! Hester !

[*Turns away ; sinking down on the moss.*

Enter HESTER, *from hut.*

Hester. Thou, Arthur,—here ?

Arthur. Who speaks ?

Hester. 'Tis I.

Arthur. Thou, truly, Hester,—here in life ?

Hester. Know'st thou me not ; so long the time
'Twixt then and now ?

Arthur I know thee well, but long is the time
'Twixt then and now,—
Since our hidden joy was in its prime;
For grief sets age upon my brow.
And thou ; ah, thou,—
Hast thou found peace ?

Hester (*pausing, shakes head and makes a gesture*).
Alas !—Or thou release ?

Arthur. Nay ; naught but despair !
What else could be mine,

Since, tho' I wander whithersoe'er,
My life is wrapt in dark deceit?

Hester. Yet still thy people reverence thee.

Arthur. Hence the greater my misery:
For Satan laughs, while my people praise.
Happy art thou, who bearest
On thy breast the Scarlet Letter.

Hester. Happy!—what dost thou say?

Arthur Ah, better, far better
To wear that raiment,
Than life-long lurk in deceit.
Woe unto me!—
My letter in secret still doth burn
With a pain that never and never dies;
As though I stood at the judgment-seat,
Nor offered even confession's payment;
While, from the throne above,
Like trumpet-blasts,
I hear the accusing voice:—
"Thou, consecrate and placed
O'er men, to teach them purity,
False art thou to thy trust!
Thy calling hast thou disgraced.
Soiled are thy robes, and thou
Liest low in the dust;
A withered bough,
That God into flame unending casts!"
Had I but one friend,
Or a foe—the worst—
To whom I might bend
Each day, and be known as a sinner vile,—
E'en so much truth might reconcile
My soul to life. But, now, each breath
Is falsehood, emptiness—death!

Hester. Such a friend thou hast—
Behold!—in me,
O'er the bitter present, the vanished past
Of thy sin and mine,
To weep, with thee.

Arthur. Ay! Friend so true,
Forgiving and tender,—
Could charity human

The wrong undo,
Then were I saved by the faith of a woman
Thro' pitying tears of rainbow splendor.

Hester. Alas, not only a friend
Serves thy behoof :
There dwells with thee under thy roof
The enemy thou dost desire ;
A foe accursed !

Arthur. What mean'st thou ? That man ;—
Gray Chillingworth ?
Thou sayest that he
My soul's deep may scan ?
Long since I felt his presence was hate,
And the grasp of his hand the clutch of fate.
But, since thou dost know,
Tell me :—why is he my foe ?

Hester. Know, then, the truth till now from thee hid :
This man of dread
Who now doth hold us both appalled—
He, Arthur, was my husband !

Arthur. Thy husband ? O hideous thought,
Beyond belief !
Woman, what wrong hast thou wrought,—
My soul to lay bare
With its anguish of sin,
That he, like a hawk of the air,
Might pierce within,
And the secret black from my bosom tear ?
Thou hast struck me a blow
None else might dare ;
And hast laid me low
In the dust at his feet.
Where now shall I turn,—
By mine enemy pent ?
No refuge, now, for my soul's distress,
Save the tangle deep of the wilderness
Wherein to hide.

[*Pause.*

Or else—ah, see !

[*Takes out a phial from within his vestments.*

Hester, herein I hold a key
To the prisoning earth.

Wide it would open the gate
To a life beyond :
For cunningly Chillingworth
This poison distilled
From herbs that give death.
Who knows if God willed,—
Or hell-born hate—
That I the potion found ?
'Tis mine ; and be it a foe or friend,
If its lips touch mine, my woe will end.

Hester (*seizes the poison-phial from him*).
No, no. It is not thine !
If freedom come,
It shall be from my lips,—
Not those of death, that strike thee dumb.
Why here abide ?
Is the world not wide ?
Nay ; bend thy steps to the path of the sea !
It bore thee hither, and so again
May carry thee hence, to make thee free.

Arthur. I *cannot* go ! No strength have I
To battle longer ;
Far, far from thee
To toil and strive new life to find.
The endless pain
Of sin unspoken my steps would track,
And fling me prone.
Ah, think !—in distant lands to wander ;
Exiled, unknown
To die !

Hester (*softly*). Thou shalt not go alone !

Arthur. Hester !

Hester. With thee I go ! We look not back,
But forth with brave endeavor.
To thee my strength I lend :
My arm will shelter, my love enfold thee.
No siren of death from me can withhold thee.
Let our hearts take wing—
As here the symbol of wrong I fling
From my breast forever !

[*Tearing off the Scarlet Letter, she throws it far from her. The white hood, dropping from her head, lets her hair fall loose.*

Strong are we and young :
Ay ; thou art so, my friend.
And dost thou not still find in me
The beauty once to thee so dear ?

Arthur. O Hester ! the glow
Of thy love my love of life renews.
Thy blood beats warm :
With thee I brave the storm !
At last we are free :
The cloud of sorrow fades far behind us,
And never the mist of the future shall blind us.

Hester. Ay ; the past is gone !
We look to the coming years ;
Since grief is done with, and dawn
Makes joy of our midnight fears.

Arthur. Thro' the forest the sunshine breaks,
In a flood of radiance rolled ;
And within us the splendor awakes
Of happiness yet untold.
Ah, Hester, the golden ray
Of hope shines bright in thine eyes.

Hester. Lo, the wings of a ship in the bay
Wait but for the winds to arise,
And waft us, with blessing divine,
Far from this land of death.

Arthur. O love ! each tone of thine
To me is heaven's breath !

Hester and Arthur.
Quick, let us haste
From the desert waste
And lingering shadows of olden sorrow,
To follow the star of a golden morrow !
The white sail gleams
With a light of dreams ;
It beckons us on with gladdening hope,
No more in anguish dark to grope.
To a land of new life.
The ship's prow speeds ;
Nor omens drear in its flight it heeds :
For grief is but foam in the sharp keel's furrow—
Quick, then, escape ! Nor cast
One glance at the stormy past !

[CURTAIN.]

ACT III.

The Market-Place, as in Act I, with view of harbor at back. A crowd of Puritan men and women, intermingled with men from forest settlements. Sailors interspersed among crowd. CHILLINGWORTH *is seen at one side, conferring closely with the Bristol Shipmaster. A crowd of English Pilgrims, just arriving at the Market-Place. During their song* CHILLINGWORTH *leaves the Shipmaster and disappears in the crowd.*

GLEE.

The new Pilgrims. From loud winds blowing,
And ocean spray,
We come to the seed-time sowing
Of Massachusetts Bay.
Then ho, to the New World, greeting;
And a hey for the pilgrim, hey!

With hope for the morrow
And every day;
Or be it for gladness or sorrow,
In New England we will stay,—
Each true man with his sweeting,—
And the law of the land obey!

Shipmaster (crossing stage). But as for me—
To the ancient island lies my way,
However wild the waves may be.
I, in sooth, myself am wild;
And yet, a faithful child,
Dear mother England I long to see.

The new Pilgrims. With a heigh for the Pilgrim, hey!

[*Music of Procession heard in distance. The crowd surges off to one side, looking for the pageant to approach.*

Chorus (*behind the scenes*). Hark! They are coming
In stately array.
Hear the music proud, the roll of the drumming.
Cheer, now, cheer for Election day.
The minister true and the new magistrate
Once more will ope to us liberty's gate,
And close it against all hardy sin.
Thank heaven we stand the gate within!

Enter HESTER.

[*Those of the people who are nearest her, shrink away.*

CHORUS.

Puritans. The sign of thy sin
A magic circle has drawn around thee;
Scorn ever shall hound thee:
Away; away!

[*They leave the stage.*

Hester. Alone? ay, gladly;
For not, as once, an outcast prone
I lie at your feet.
My freedom I greet,
And move apart—no longer sadly!
No longer to you a bond-slave I moan,
Nor dark spells now my soul defile.
On the Scarlet Letter look your last!
For, yet a little while,
Your tyrant sway is past.
Tho' now I must yield,
There in the forest vast
The blight from my bosom I cast:
If here I endure it again,
To triumph is turned this outward stain—
On the joy, that throbs within me, sealed.
Soon, soon beyond your reach,
Harsh people merciless,
I fly to the whispering tide
And the loved one's caress.
Yon dark mysterious sea will hide
My wrong and my happiness
From your evil speech!

[*To the Shipmaster, who has come near her.*

God greet thee! All is well?

Shipmaster. Ay, mistress; if I dare say so!
I have it on truth of a witch's word;
And witches, I've heard,
Know darkness from light.
Our barque is ready:
At anchor she rides
For a turn of the tides:
And, wind holding steady,
We sail to-night.
Good omen I deem it,
And company rare,
That you, sweet lady,
With us will fare.

Hester. Dost thou not know
The best of omens thou canst hope
Will be his presence who goes with me?

Shipmaster. Is it truly so?
Then darkly I grope.
Didst thou not say he flies in fear
Of hurt from the Puritan Fathers here?
If wrong he has wrought,
How can his presence with blessing be fraught?
Still—the better, say I, if saint he be!
Since thou spokest, last night,
Of passage flight,
Yon old leech came to seek a berth.
He, too, it seems, would cross the earth.
If saint and doctor together go,
Fair winds indeed must blow.

Hester (aside). Ah, worse than death those words presage!
[*To Shipmaster*
Yon leech! What mean you?

Shipmaster. Why, he—the old chirurgeon mage:
Know you not?—Chillingworth.

Hester. Then he, too, has seen you?
Dost tell me now, that he will sail
With us on your ship?

Shipmaster. Ay; with a favoring gale
And gladsome weather,
To these bitter folk we'll give the slip.
Is it not well done?

He,—the hump-shouldered one—
Long has he known your friend :
They've dwelt together.
The leech will cling to him unto the end.

[*He leaves her and mingles with the crowd.*

Hester. Lost, lost, then. All is lost !
Nor in this New World solitude,
Or amid-sea tossed,
Can we the black enchantment elude !

[*She perceives* CHILLINGWORTH *at the opposite side of the market-place, smiling at her with vindictive meaning.*

O devil-face and mocking smile !
Where watchful malice ever lurks !—
What serpent in that heart of guile
So sombre dwells and slyly works,—
Sharp gleaming on me from his eyes ?
Our plot he unriddles ; our hope forestalls,
With craft unknown.
Closer he holds us than prison-walls :
Hate is harder than stone.
Ah, if unto Arthur
One word of warning
I might but speak !
Yet, alas, 'mid the multitude scorning,
The sole one who loves me I dare not seek.
Help, help ! Will God not find us,
'Mid the snares of hell that bind us ?

[*Music of procession heard nearer.*

Chill. (*on opposite side of market-place*).
In vain the wile
Of flight or turning ;
And wasted all her woeful cries !
For unto my hate, like incense burning,
Her flame of agony still doth rise.
The last word is spoken ;
Her last hope broken ;
Her with her lover henceforth I hold
In the mesh of my net.
They shall render me yet

A heavier price of their wrong, than gold.
And what can their anguish weigh
'Gainst the hurt to my hidden pride?
Or go they or stay,
My vengeance they still must abide,
And in torture burn;—
For all entreating of pity I spurn.

Chorus (*behind the scenes*).

How gayly they play!
They know the tune for Election Day.

[*Enter Band of Musicians, from one side, followed by the populace.*

Chorus. The Company Ancient
Of Honored Artillery!

[*Enter escort of Citizen Soldiers—the Ancient and Honorable Artillery Company—in burnished steel, with gay plumes nodding over their morions.*

Chorus And the magistrates! Lo,
They come with fitting footsteps slow.

Enter BELLINGHAM.

Chorus. Thou who wast governor,—
Praised be thy skill!
But now we greet our new ruler,
The choice of the people's will.
Beat loud the drums!
John Endicott comes.
Endicott! Endicott!—
Governor elect!

[*Enter, during this chorus,* GOVERNOR JOHN ENDICOTT, *accompanied by other dignitaries, and bows to the crowd, right and left.* BELLINGHAM, ENDICOTT *and the others arrange themselves near Church, at back.*

Chorus. Behold our pastor—
Dear Master Arthur.
And yet his face—how pale!
A shadow sable
Draws round him as he advances.

Nay :. these are fancies ;
For see how firm, erect
He steps,—as though some purpose high
His weakness were sustaining.
God-given impulse only, past all fear,
Could guide his forces frail
To bring us here
His treasure of teaching,
And bounteous preaching—
Sweet thoughts upon us raining.
Welcome, our pastor : hail—
Our hope that cannot fail !

[*Enter* ARTHUR, *with* WILSON.

BELLINGHAM, ENDICOTT *and the others wait for* ARTHUR *to approach the Church, through the lane which they have formed.*

ARTHUR, *standing erect, yet apparently weak physically, pauses. Then, instead of going towards the Church, he turns ; crosses the stage slowly, and beckons to* HESTER.

Arthur. Hester, come hither :
My Hester——come !

[HESTER, *who till now has remained where she was, half crouching in despair, draws herself up and moves towards him slowly, as if spell-bound.*

Chill. (*starting forth from the crowd*).
Hold, madman ! Hold !
What dreams distraught
Your senses benumb !
Wave back that woman !
I yet can save you :
All shall be well.

Arthur. Ha, tempter appalling,
Thou art too late !
Thy power no longer
My life controls :
A spirit stronger
Than thine quells thy hate.
God is mighty above us. The soul of souls
My will at last sets free from thine :
I shall escape thee now !

Chorus. What trouble does Satan for us design ?
Some phantasy strange, pursuing
The blameless mind, his reason has shaken !

Arthur. Come, Hester Prynne,
Thou who knowest my sin ;
Ay, Hester, come in His name,
So terrible, yet in mercy so mild,
Who has granted me grace
At the final hour to proclaim
My wickedness here, and face to face,
The evil so long within bemoaned,
But never owned,
Aloud to speak.
Thy offered strength around me twine ;
But let it obey the will divine !
Ah, Hester, I need thee ;
For stricken, weary and weak,
Now at the end,
Tho' it be but with steps of a little child,—
Yon scaffold with thee will I ascend.

[*He points to the Pillory, taking* HESTER'S *hand. The People murmur, but are dazed, and dare not interpose, as* ARTHUR *and* HESTER *move towards the Pillory, and mount it.* CHILLINGWORTH *follows them to the steps.*

Bellingham. Some witchcraft, I fear,
Or spirit impure,
His mind doth deceive.
Thou, Father Wilson,
The devil adjure
That in peace our Arthur he leave.

Wilson. Arthur, Arthur, this magic forsake :
To thy true self awake !

Arthur (*standing with* HESTER *on Pillory*).
O people of New England !
Ye still who love me,
And holy have deemed me !
Your pastor behold,
Not as you long have dreamed me,
But, as heaven shines high above me,—

So of all sinners the lowest.
Thou shalt reap as thou sowest!
From falsehood's seed
I garner disgrace:
But, lo, I uproot the shriveled weed,
And the flower of truth blooms here, in its place!
The Scarlet Letter that Hester wears—
Ye have shuddered at, long:
But its lurid ray
Was but as a shadow of that fierce fire
Of smothered wrong
That, night and day,
With flaming despairs
My breast has scarred, and branded my soul!
Her fellow in sin, I have won my desire
And reached my goal;
For I stand now beside her,
The debt of my guilt's confession to pay,
So long denied her.
If any here still
God's judgment deny,
Here now ere I die
Let them witness his will
In the blood-red mark revealed on my breast:
The Scarlet Letter—behold!

[*Tears away the ministerial band from before his breast, and sinks backward, supported by Hester.*

Chorus. O wonder! Weird and awful sign!
Saw you the living token
Baleful blazing, over his heart
Tracing its fearful sanguine line?
If truth he has spoken—
Ah, pity accord!
Arthur we praised,
And Hester abhorred:
So far we kept them in thought apart:
Yet now, amazed,
Together we see them brought,
In the chain of justice God hath wrought.

Chill. (*crouching in despair on the Pillory steps*).

Thou hast escaped me !
Hadst thou sought the whole world over,
No place or high or lowly
Couldst thou have found
Wherein to baffle me wholly,—
Save this mean scaffold's bound !

Hester. O Arthur, look not afar from me !
Here close am I, and my love replies
To the light of thine eyes.
Turn thou not away !
Ah, whither, then, does thy spirit stray ?

Arthur. To the land of the fountain unending
Of peace my soul is wending,
Where sorrow ne'er draws breath.
Ay, far to wander we planned,
Dear Hester—thou and I—
To a foreign strand.
But now I voyage beyond the sky—
To that home I seek, the land
Of death !

Hester. Wait, Arthur ! Wait!
For dost thou not remember,
I told thee in the forest
Thou shalt not go alone ?

[ARTHUR *sighs, looks at her longingly, then dies.*

Ha ! Hast thou fled me,—
So swiftly gone ?
My dearest one—O soul beloved ?

[*Takes out from her bosom the poison phial.*

Thee, then, I'll follow ! The poignant draught
Brewed by our enemy's fateful craft,
Will give me release.
Thou, too, dear Arthur,
Didst from it seek freedom ;
And I sought to save thee.

'Twill save me from life :
And sweet to my lips its coldness comes,
As the cool winds that blow
From mountains white forever with snow.
Thou shalt not go alone !

[*She drinks the poison and dies.*

Chorus. Hush, hush ! Their souls are fled.
Peace unto the dead !
The flower of sacrifice
Blooms in no earthly garden.
Thou, Hester, over us triumph hast won ;
Towards mercy turning our sullen hate.
Thou, Arthur, though repenting late,—
May God thee pardon !

[End of the Scarlet Letter.]

The Scarlet Letter.

Opera in three Acts

by

Walter Damrosch.

Op. 1.

Words by George Parsons Lathrop after Hawthorne's Romance.

Vocal Score by the Composer.

Breitkopf & Härtel,
Leipzig · Brussels · London · New York ·

21181.

This work is dedicated
to my wife
Margaret Blaine.

The Scarlet Letter.

Opera in three Acts

by

WALTER DAMROSCH.

Op. 1.

Words by George Parsons Lathrop
after Hawthorne's Romance.

Vocal Score by the Composer.

Persons Represented.

Arthur	Tenore.	**Bellingham**	Basso.
Hester	Soprano.	**Brackett**	Basso.
Chillingworth	Baritone.	**A Shipmaster**	Basso.
Wilson	Basso.		

First Act.

(The Market-Place, Boston, with Prison at L., a rosebush in bloom growing by the door. At back, a Church or Meeting-House. At R., the Town-Hall, and near it the Pillory, R.C. Openings on either side of the Meeting-House, giving a view of Boston Harbor.

Puritan men and women, entering through these streets and at sides, assemble in excitement.

Master Brackett, the Jailer, with a company of Soldiers, stands near the Prison door.)

Stich und Druck von Breitkopf & Härtel in Leipzig.
21181

Soprano.
How bold - ly shines the
Alto.
How bold - ly shines the
CORO I.
Tenore.
How bold - ly shines the sun
Basso.
How bold - ly shines the sun
Soprano.
How
Alto.
How
CORO II.
Tenore.
How bold - - ly
Basso.
How bold - - ly

21181

sun
yet out - er dark - - - - ness en -
sun
yet out - er dark - - ness en -
yet out - er dark - - - ness en - folds you
yet out - er dark - - - ness en - folds you
bold - ly shines the sun yet out - er dark - ness en -
bold - ly shines the sun yet out - er dark - ness en -
shines the sun yet out - er dark - ness en -
shines the sun yet out - er dark - ness en -
dim.
f

folds you wick - ed wom - - an.
folds you wick - ed wom - - an.
wick - - ed wom - - an. How
wick - - ed wom - - an. How
folds you wick - ed wom - - an. How
folds you wick - ed wom - - an. How
folds you wick - ed wom - - an. How bold - ly shines the
folds you wick - ed wom - - an. How bold - ly shines the

21181

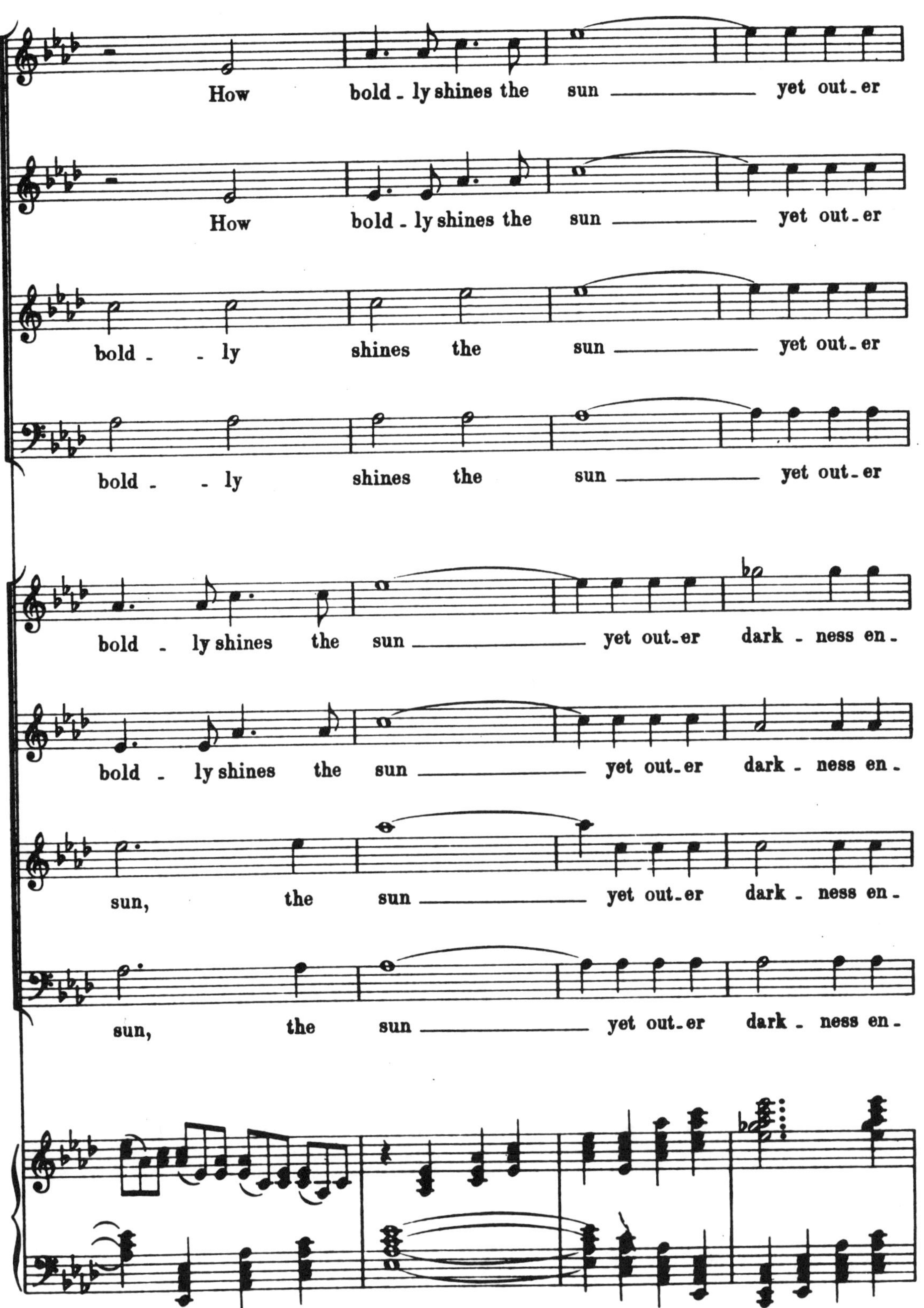
How bold - ly shines the sun yet out - er
How bold - ly shines the sun yet out - er
bold - - ly shines the sun yet out - er
bold - - ly shines the sun yet out - er
bold - ly shines the sun yet out - er dark - ness en -
bold - ly shines the sun yet out - er dark - ness en -
sun, the sun yet out - er dark - ness en -
sun, the sun yet out - er dark - ness en -

dark - ness en - folds you wick-ed wom - an, yet out-er
dark - ness en - folds you wick-ed wom - an, yet out-er
dark - ness en - folds you wick-ed wom - an, yet out-er
dark - ness en - folds you wick-ed wom - an, yet out-er
folds you wick - ed wom - an, en -
folds you wick - ed wom - an, en -
folds you wick - ed wom - an, en -
folds you wick - ed wom - an, en -
f

21131

darkness enfolds you wicked wom - an.
darkness enfolds you wicked wom - an.
darkness enfolds you wicked wom - an. While within her,
darkness enfolds you wicked wom - an. While within her,
folds you wick - ed wom - an.
folds you wick - ed wom - an.
folds you wick - ed wom - an. While with - in her the
folds you wick - ed wom - an. While with - in her the

while within her the wrong that she has done gleams bold as bale-fire
while within her the wrong that she has done gleams bold as bale-fire
wrong that she has done gleams bold as bale - fire 'gainst the light of
wrong that she has done gleams bold as bale - fire 'gainst the light of

While within her the wrong that she has done gleams bold as bale - fire

While within her the wrong that she has done gleams bold as bale - fire

'gainst the light of day,

'gainst the light of day,

While within her the wrong that she has done gleams

While within her the wrong that she has done gleams

day, while within her the

day, while within her the

21181

'gainst the light of day. O child of er - ror,
'gainst the light of day. O child of er - ror,
'gainst the light of day. O child of er - ror,
'gainst the light of day. O child of er - ror,
bold as bale - fire 'gainst the light of day. O child of
bold as bale - fire 'gainst the light of day. O child of
wrong that she has done gleams bold 'gainst the light of day. O child of
wrong that she has done gleams bold 'gainst the light of day. O child of

21181

fair,_ caught in your beau - ty's own unhallow'd snare,
fair,_ caught in your beau - ty's own unhallow'd snare,
fair, caught in your beau - ty's own unhallow'd snare,
fair, caught in your beau - ty's own unhallow'd snare,
er - ror fair, caught in your beau - ty's own unhallow'd
er-ror fair, caught in your beau - ty's own unhallow'd
er - ror fair, caught in your beau - ty's own unhallow'd
er - ror fair, caught in your beau - ty's own unhallow'd
3

O child of er - ror fair,
O child of er - ror fair,
O child of er - ror fair,
O child of er - ror fair,
snare, O child of er - ror fair, caught in your
snare, O child of er - ror fair, caught in your
snare, O child of er - ror fair, caught in your
snare, O child of er - ror fair, caught in your

caught in your beau - ty's own unhallow'd snare.
caught in your beau - ty's own unhallow'd snare.
caught in your beau - ty's own unhallow'd snare.
caught in your beau - ty's own unhallow'd snare.
beau - ty's own unhallow'd snare.
beau - ty's own unhallow'd snare.
beau - ty's own unhallow'd snare.
beau - ty's own unhallow'd snare.

How bold-ly shines the sun
How bold-ly shines the sun
How bold - ly shines the sun to
How bold - ly shines the sun to
How bold-ly shines the sun to
How bold-ly shines the sun to
How bold-ly shines the sun to flare up-
How bold-ly shines the sun to flare up-

21181

to flare up-on her shame. How boldly
to flare up-on her shame. How boldly
flare up - - on her shame. How bold - ly
flare up - - on her shame. How bold - ly
flare upon her shame. How bold-ly shines the
flare upon her shame. How bold-ly shines the
on her shame. How bold - ly shines the sun
on her shame. How bold - ly shines the sun

shines the sun to flare up - on
shines the sun to flare up , on
shines the sun to flare up - - on
shines the sun to flare up - - on
sun to flare up-on her shame.
sun to flare up-on her shame.
to flare up - on her shame.
to flare up - on her shame.

21121

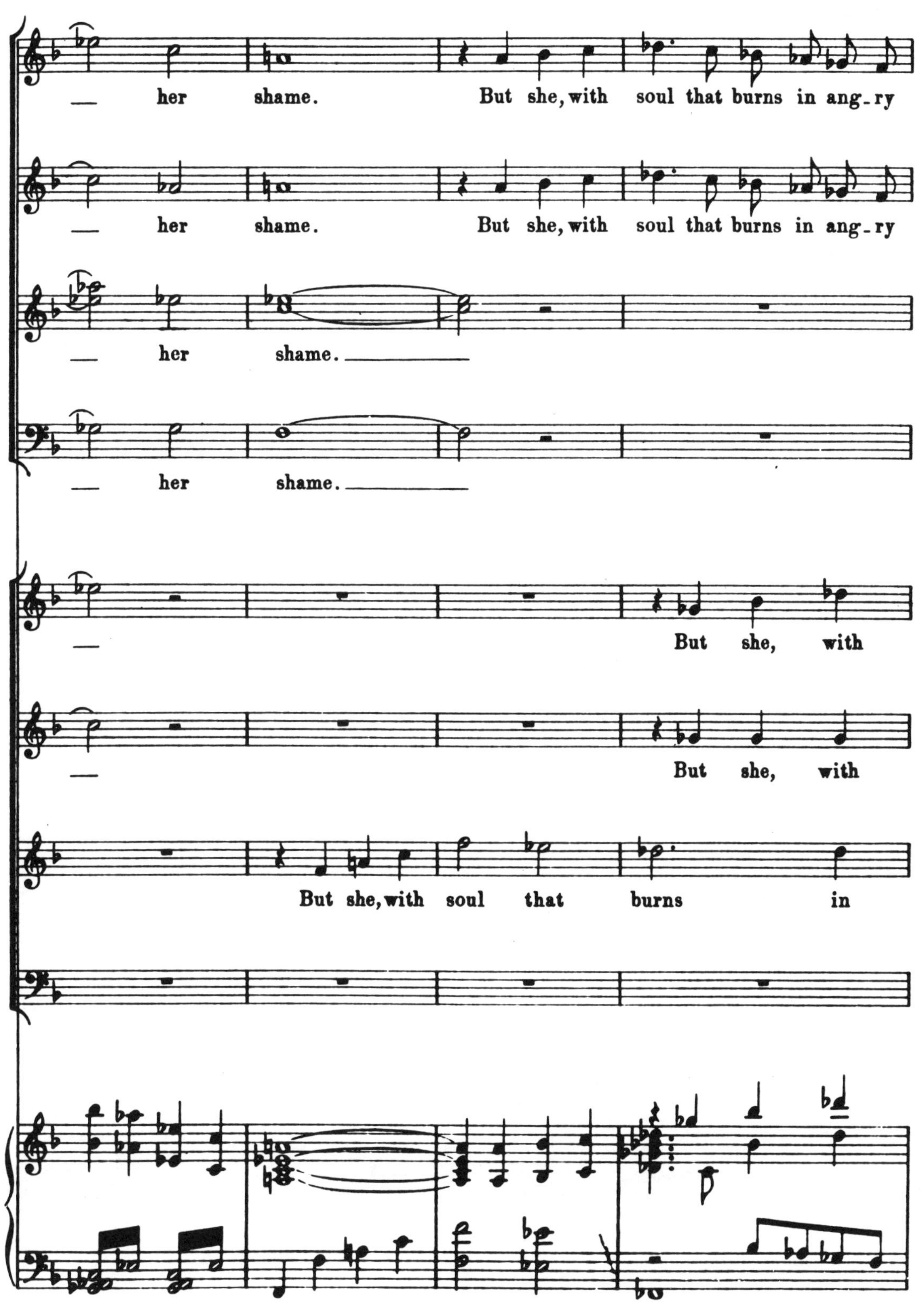
— her shame. But she, with soul that burns in ang-ry
— her shame. But she, with soul that burns in ang-ry
— her shame.
— her shame.
— But she, with
— But she, with
But she, with soul that burns in

flame. but she, with soul that burns in ang-ry
flame, but she, with soul that burns in
But she, with soul that burns in ang - - - ry
But she, with soul that burns in angry flame,
soul that burns in ang-ry flame, hides
soul that burns in ang - ry flame, hides
ang - ry flame, hides
hides

flame, hides close in her pris - on. Bring her
ang-ry flame, quick bring her forth, bring her
flame, hides close in her pris - on, Bring her
quick bring her forth, bring her
close in her pris - on. Quick bring her forth, bring her
close in her pris - on. Quick bring her forth, bring her
close in her pris - on. Quick bring her forth, bring her
close in her pris - on. Quick bring her forth, bring her

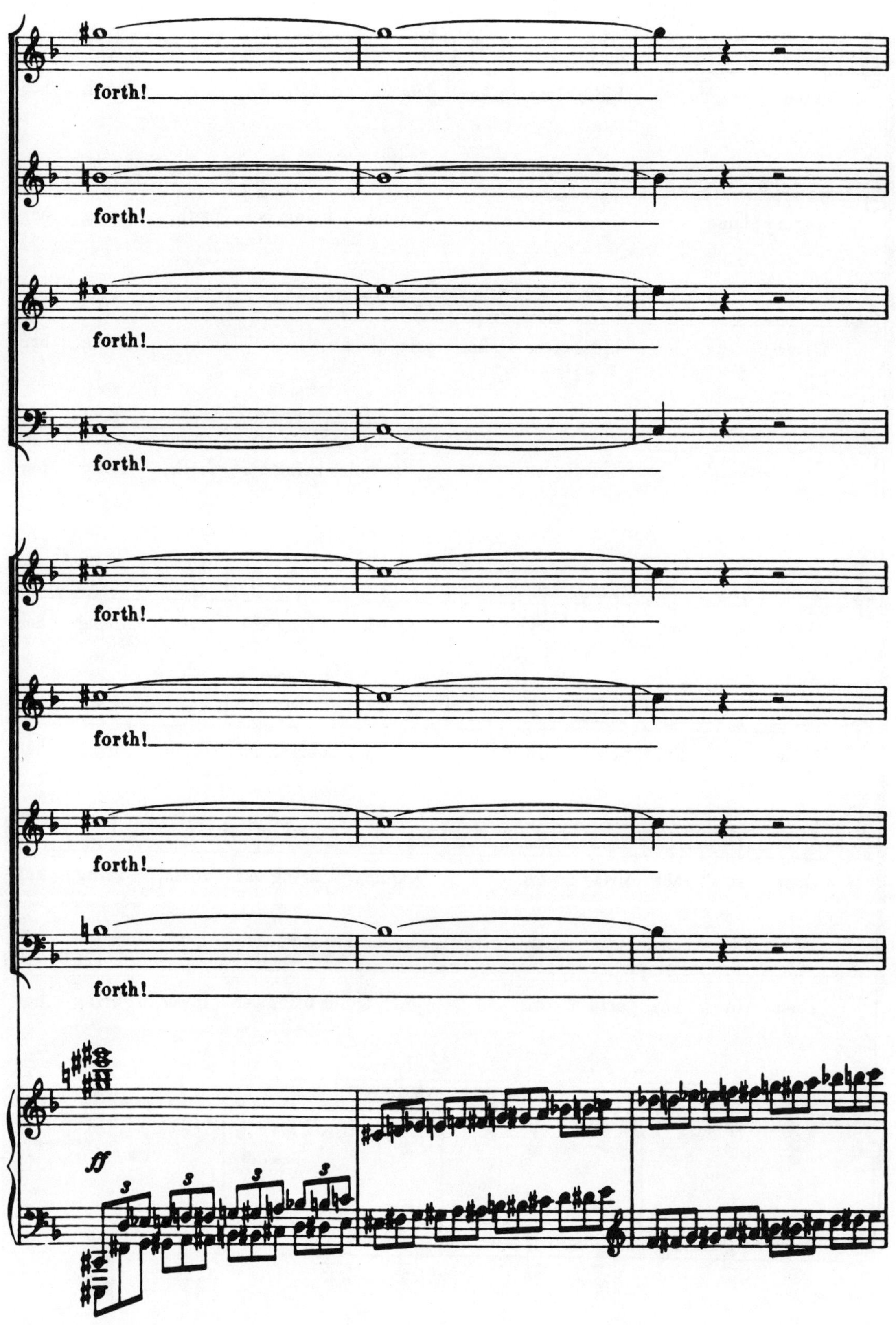
forth!
forth!
forth!
forth!
forth!
forth!
forth!
forth!
ff
3
3
3
3

(The crowd surge against the door of the prison but are driven back by Brackett and the soldiers.)

21181

(Pushing aside
Br.
ju - stice, then, at his hands.
the people.)
Br.
A - side there, stand a - side I say,
Sopr.
CORO.
Alto.
Quick bring her forth, bring her forth.
Ten.
Bass.
Quick bring her forth, bring her forth.
Br.
you blust - er like the wind, for your will is like the
The wo - man has foul - ly sinned,
The wo - man has foul - ly sinned,
cresc.

Br.
winds rough way.
bring her forth, the wo - man has foul - ly
bring her forth, the wo - man has foul - ly
ff
dim.
cresc.
sinned, yet ju - stice slumb - ers,
slumb - ers, ju - stice
sinned, yet ju - stice slumb - ers,
ff
Ped.
To our folk she must ex - pi -
slumb - ers.
To our folk she must ex - pi -
ff

brought ___ on them.
ate the wrong she has brought on them.
ate the wrong she has brought on them.
Soprano.
If she stood here before us for pit - y or par - don to sue and im -
Alto.
Tenore.
If she stood here before us for pit - y or par - don to
Basso.
If she
CORO.

plore us, no mer - cy would

If she stood here be-fore us to sue and im -

sue and im - plore us, sue and im-plore us,—

stood here be-fore us for sue and im - plore us, no

light - en her burden, no mer-cy would light-en her bur - den.

plore us, no mer-cy would light - - en her bur - den.

no mer-cy would light - en her bur-den.

mer - cy would light - en her bur - - den. For

To crime give its guerdon.
For judg - ment stern we would render.
To crime give its guerdon. To crime give its
judg - ment stern, for judg - ment stern we would rend - - -
Her sin is ab - hor - - rent.
Her sin is ab - hor - - - rent.
guerdon. Her sin is ab - horrent. Her
er. Her sin is ab - hor - - - -

Her sin is ab - hor - rent.
Her sin is ab_hor_rent.
sin is ab_horrent. Her sin is ab_hor_rent.
rent. Her sin, her sin is ab_hor_rent.
Death's doom we would a - ward her,
Death's doom we would a - ward her,
Death's doom we would a - ward her,
Death's doom we would a - ward her,
ff

since the law gives us war - - - rant
since the law gives us war - - - rant
since the law gives us war - - - rant
since the law gives us war - - - rant
to judgment, to judgment, to judg - - ment.
to judgment, to judgment, to judg - - ment.
to judgment, to judgment, to judg - - ment.
to judgment, to judgment, to judg - - ment.

(They make another rush at the gail but are driven back by the soldiers, who gradually open a lane from the prison-door to the scaffold.)

ff

fff furioso

dim. poco

a poco

Andante. Chillingworth (who enters unobserved)

What wrathful sound is this that rises loud?

C.

How fierce their anger 'gainst an erring soul! — O

strange, tho' oft I've heard the hungry storm roar for its pray; sharp winds of

espressivo *cresc.* *poco*

ocean moan - ing, more dread - ful, more dread - ful

a *poco* *mf* *cresc. ed accel.*

is this cry — of hu - man hearts —

un poco

(The prison door opens. Crowd subsides into momentary hush. In the dark shadow of the corridor withon the prison door a red glow is seen proceeding from a lantern hanging there. The soldiers form a lane through the crowd from the prison door to the pillory.)

Più allegro.

CORO I.

Behold, she comes!

Behold, she comes!

CORO II.

Be - hold, she comes!

Be - hold, she comes!

Più allegro.

p

f

Coro I e II.

p

Hush, hush, be - hold, from the prison gleams a

p

Hush, hush, be - hold, from the prison gleams a

fp

p

(Enter from prison-door a jailer followed after a brief pause by **Hester**. She stands for a moment on the door-step, silent, dignified, yet woe-begone. Hester, accompanied by **Brackett**, crosses stage towards the pillory. Some of the crowd point at the Scarlet Letter on her breast. Others turn away or shield their eyes as though horror-stricken and blinded by it.)

Chill. (roused by their cries, moves tho where he can see Hester, and gazes at her, at first curiously).

This creature who? Nay— what hor - ror, my wife!
fp
f

(Hester walks slowly along the lane formed by the soldiers towards the pillory.)
Andante grave.
C.
my wife!
CORO I.
Je_ze_bel!
Je_ze_bel!
CORO II.
Je_ze_bel!
Je_ze_bel!
Andante grave.
ff
daughter of Hell! See! See, how ser_pent_like it
daughter of Hell! See! See, how ser_pent_like it
daughter of Hell! See,___ how ser_pent_like it
daughter of Hell! See,___ how ser_pent_like it
21181

twines, yon let - ter, with its coil - ing lines,
twines, yon let - ter, with its coil - ing lines,
twines, yon let - ter, with its coil - ing lines, as
twines, yon let - ter, with its coil - ing lines, as
as though it were clutch - ing her breast of her soul in
as though it were clutch - ing her breast of her soul in
though it were clutch - ing her breast of her soul in quest.
though it were clutch - ing her breast of her soul in quest.

quest. Lo, she sports with her shame and has
quest. Lo, she sports with her shame and has
Lo, she sports with her shame and has wov - en the
Lo, she sports with her shame and has wov - en the
ff
wov - en the let - ter with gau - dy splend - or of
wov - en the let - ter with gau - dy splend - or of
let - ter with gau - dy splend - or of
let - ter with gau - dy splend - or of

(Brackett and the Soldiers
scar - - - - let. The tok - en, that
scar - - - - let. The tok - en, that
scar - let. The tok - en that should be her fet - ter she
scar - let. The tok - en that should be her fet - ter she
8
sff
protect Hester from crowd. Reaching Pillory, she ascends it, and stands alone there, defiant.)
should be her fet - ter she turns to a flame of a - dorn - ment.
should be her fet - ter she turns to a flame of a - dorn - ment.
turns to a mocking flame of a - dorn - ment.
turns to a mocking flame of a - dorn - ment.
8

21181

Allegro tempestoso.
CORO.
Down with the curs - ed har - lot, down with the curs - ed har - lot,
Down with the curs - ed har - lot, down with the curs - ed har - lot,
Allegro tempestoso.
down with the curs- - - -ed har - lot! Down with the cursed har-lot,
down with the curs- - - -ed har - lot! Down with the cursed har-lot,
down with the cursed har-lot, down with the curs - - - -ed har - lot!
down with the cursed har-lot, down with the curs - - - -ed har - lot!

Chill.

C. O blasting mock - e - ry, o bleak des-

Pun-ish her ev - il do-ing,

Pun - ish her ev - il do-ing,

Pun-ish her ev - il do-ing,

Pun - ish her ev - il

C. pair! All merc - y with-ers now in fires of

Ban - ish her shad-ow that dark - ens each Pu-ri-tan dwel-ling,

...each Pu-ri-tan dwel-ling,

Ban-ish her shad-ow that dark - ens each Pu-ri-tan

do-ing. stain-ing us all with dis-

C.
p
hate and from my heart
stain-ing us all with dis-hon-or, tempt-ing God's
stain-ing us all with dis - hon - - or,
dwel - - ling, stain-ing us all with dis - hon - or,
hon - or, tempt - ing God's
C.
— like black - est vap- - - - - - - ors rolls
wrath in dis - ast - - er.
tempt - - ing God's wrath in dis - ast - - er.
tempt - - ing God's wrath in dis - ast - - er.
wrath in dis - ast - - er.

rit. un poco
C.
up like black - - - - - est vapor!
Far in-to Hell - fire cast her.
Far in-to Hell - fire cast her.
Far in-to Hell - fire cast her.
Far in-to Hell - fire cast her.
rit. un poco
a tempo
C.
Rev-enge!
Down with the cursed har-lot, down with the cursed har-lot, down with the curs -
Down with the cursed har-lot, down with the cursed har-lot, down with the curs -
ff a tempo

ed har_lot, down!
ed har_lot, down!
ff

(Drum roll heard. Enter on the balcony of the Town - Hall, **Arthur Dimmesdale**, with his senior colleague, **Rev. John Wilson**, **Gov. Bellingham** and other dignitaries, attended by four sergeants.)

f
Drum on the stage.
f
f
dim.

(**Arthur** fixes his gaze on **Hester**, who answers him with a glance full of meaning.)

Wilson (rising).
Hest - er Prynne! Heark - - en! Thy
p
f
p
W.
husband absent far beyond the sea; a child to thee here was born
p
p
cresc.
p
Allegro.
W.
bringing dis - grace and scorn
cresc. ed accel.
sf
ff
Ped.
rit.
dim.
rit.
Tempo I.
W.
Heaven's wise de - cree has tak - en thy daught - er a - way
espressivo
mf
R.H.
pesante

W.
waft - ed on wings of death.
cresc.
con espressione
Andante con moto.
If with her thou wouldst feel heavn's hol-y breath, no
p
long-er thy se-cret con-ceal, but— thy fel-low of-
cresc. poco a poco
fend - - er ac-cuse!
f
cresc.
ff
dim.

(Hester remains silent.)
W.
Hast thou no word to say?
Dost thou re_fuse?
p
mf
dim.
p
(Arthur clutches his hands to his heart as if to master his a-gitation.)
(Hester is still silent.)
pp dolce
trem.
agitato ed un poco piu vivo
mf
dim.
p rit.
Tempo I.
Wilson (to Hester, laying his hand on Arthur's shoulder.)
With my brother I've striv_en, my col_league and pastor, this god_ly
p
W.
youth, that here in the face of heav'n he deal with you,

W.
touching the truth that no long-er you hide his name who wrought you this
cresc. e accel. poco a poco
wrong and let to your griev - ous— fall - ing
guiltburd - ened, bow your pride of sin.
f
Hear con - science call - ing.
acceler.
8
ff

Allegro risoluto.
Bellingham (to Arthur).
Yea, worthy sir, you are her past - or and preacher,
speak with her, plead, ex-horst, beseech her. Tho' thou hast
wand - er'd far from the true path stray - ing; the ev-il is in the
deed, not in the say - ing. Therefore take heed! con-
Be.
fp
f

Be.

fess! con-fess! and the

dim.

(to Arthur)

Be.

powers of heav-en may bless thy late re-lent-ing. But

fp

Be.

you o gent-le broth-er, a-lone can prove if she have

p espress.

Un poco più lento.

Be.

grace for re pent-ing. This hap-less mother lost wife be-

rit.
Be.
guiled_ by al_ien love, whom fate holds far from her husband and
(tenderly)
death despoils of her child.
CORO.
Yea, worthy one deal thou with this
wom - an's soul.
p un poco più vivo
mf cresc.
Ped.

(with great inner emotion)
Arthur.
Thou hear-est them,
A.
Hest-er Prynne,
and a-las thou seest the
A.
maze of grief where-in I walk, the least of those who

A.
dare sin-ners up - braid. Thy wel-fare was in my
dolce
pp
keep - ing, and so thy sin must be mine. Fully thou hadst faith in thy
guide All the more there-fore im - plor - - ing
yea weep - - - ing
p
p
cresc.

21181

A.

My pray - er must for par - don as - cend, why, then

ff

Con Ped.

A.

dost thou make no sign? Nay think,

ff

A.

if thy lips thou - hard - en, then I

mf

p *cresc.*

A.

for thy soul's sake that I so

pp *dolce*

A. care for ev-en death would dare for thy burd-en of

A. sil-ence up-on me take.

rit. a tempo

CORO.

p O wise and child - - like, sim-ple and

p O wise and child - - like, sim-ple and

rit. a tempo

p

pure with the words of an ang-el he speaks.

pure with the words of an ang-el he speaks.

p *mf*

21181

(to Hester)

A. No! Not so.

cresc.

f

A. But of one who seeks to save thee from

f *p*

A. dole. If

A. rest to thee it would give, and thy spir - it make

p

21181

A.
whole, or hope of sal-vation in-sure,
dim.
A.
tell his name who with thee now suf-fers, tho'
p
mf marcato
A.
hid-ing his guilt-y heart. High or low, spare him not from the
sf
cresc.
A.
ban. Be not too tender nor pit-y rend-

A.
er to him who so may be tempt - - -
p
cresc.
- ed to play the dis-semb - lers part.
ff
8va bassa
Remem-ber, he is not ex - - empt-ed from the
dim.
doom that ov - er - shad - - ow's thee.

A.
Think, ere thou replì - est; for
mf
cresc.
A.
ritard.
if the truth thou de-ni - est.
L.H.
ritard. e dim.
a tempo
A.
O Hest - - - - er,
a.tempo
pp dolce
rit
A.
rit.
Hest - - - er, his soul with thine condemned may
rit. e cresc.
f
ritard.
f

a tempo

(Arthur sinks back exhausted, with hand over heart. Bellingham and Wilson anxious support him.)

A. be.

CORO.

Look, look he reels, he trembles. Too sharp the

Look, look he reels, he trem - bles. Too sharp the

a tempo

f

stress of pain that he feels for the wanton's woe. Piu allegro. Tho' fallen

stress of pain that he feels for the wanton's woe. Tho' fallen

ff Piu allegro.

proud of the

low, thou shouldst be proud of the wretched-ness his

low, thou shouldst be proud of the wretched-ness

58
pit - y deigns to bless.
pit - y deigns to bless.
A.
Ay
An - swer him a - loud!
An - swer him a - loud!
cresc.
ff
ff
A.
tell them who tempt - ed thee!
dim poco
a poco
ritard. poco a poco
21181

Hester. Andante.
From me the world will nev-er know his name.
espress.
ppp
p
mf
pp
Più vivo.
Wilson.
Con-fess-ion and re-pentance may a-vail to
pp
W.
take the scarlet letter of thy breast.
f
rit.
Andante.
Hester (looking at Arthur).
It is too deep-ly bran-ded ye can-not take it
espressivo

Allegro agitato.

H. off!

Arthur.

Speak out the name!

CORO.

f Speak, — speak!

f Speak, — speak!

Allegro agitato.

fp *cresc.* *f*

Chillingworth (Fiercely).

Ay, wom - - - an, speak and give thy

fp *cresc.* *mf*

C. child a fath - - - er!

f

Hester (startled and agitated).
Ha! that voice! No! no! thrice no! My
cresc.e poco rit.
Andante grandioso.
H.
child has found it's heav'n-ly father, ye shall nev-er know its earth - - ly
f
f
Allegro agitato.
H.
one.
Arthur.
O
Chillingworth.
Then if she will not speak, Hell close her
Bellingham.
She will not speak, 'tis death with-in her soul that makes her
Wilson.
She will not speak,
Allegro agitato.
f
mf
21181

A.
mar - - vel!
She will not speak,
C.
lips but o - - pen her heart to
Be.
dumb,
she will not speak
W.
she will not speak
CORO.
She will not speak.
She will not speak.
A.
O
won - - drous kind - - ness
C.
me.
She will not speak. What here a - mong us
She will not speak. What here a - mong us

A. of a wom - - an's heart!

shall we then cher - - ish Sa - - tan's seed?

shall we then cher - - ish Sa - - tan's seed?

Nay, from the land let her per - - - ish. Ay

Nay, from the land let her per - - - ish. Ay

give her death!

give her death!

Andante con moto.
Wilson.
espressivo
Yet not in vain may pit - y
ay, give her death!
ay, give her death!
Andante con moto.
fp espressivo
Con Ped.
Arthur.
O won - drous kindness of a wom - an's heart!
Chillingworth.
Thou who
W.
seek to wake a-gain, a - gain the soul from

A. Re - proach to my soul and a - gony

C. hast be - tray'd my sac - red trust, to me thou shalt a -

W. trance its slumb - - - ers im -

A. deep! For while I keep my

C. tone ven - geance is just, ay ven - geance is

W. bu - - - ing.

Più moto.

A. se - cret a - part, she a - las, un - de - fend - ed

C. just, and in vain all con-cealing, the

Più moto.

A.
C.
CORO.
this op - en scorn a - lone must en-
trait - or un-known at my
Worship-ful Gover-nor dal-ly not long,
Worship-ful Gover-nor dal-ly not long,
dure.
feet shall be laid
dal-ly not long with her stubborn wrong. Worship-ful Governor
dal-ly not long with her stubborn wrong. Worship-ful Governor

Hester.
Maddening sil - ence, tor-ture ac -
A.
Maddening sil - ence,
C.
him - self to me re- -veal - - - - ing.
dal - ly not long with her stubborn wrong.
dal - ly not long with her stubborn wrong.
fp
3
H.
curst that burns the soul like lips a - thirst where hell - fires
A.
tor - ture ac - curst that burns the soul like lips a - thirst where

H.
roll, where hell - fi - res roll.
A.
hell - fires roll, where hell - fires roll.
rallent.
Un poco ritenuto.
H.
Ah! were this tor-ture end - - - ed!
A.
Ah! were this tor-ture end - - - ed!
Chillingworth.
To me thou shalt a -
To death!
To death!
Un poco ritenuto.

H.
Ah! were this tor-ture end - - - - - ed!
A.
Ah! were this tor-ture end - - - - - ed!
C.
tone!
Bellingham.
Though we slay her, still lives the
To death!
To death!
dim.
mf
Più vivo.
Bc.
fath - er, we vain - ly have sought.
Wilson.
Yet not in
But swift un - to death, but swift un - to
But swift un - to death,
Più vivo.
sempre agitato
cresc. poco a poco

Be.
– Young, fair, of her
W.
vain may pit - - - y seek to wake a -
death, but swift un - to death, but swift un - to
but swift un - to death, but swift un - to death,
Be.
hus - band for - sak - - - - - en, so was her
W.
gain her soul from trance
death, un - to death! Alto. Give thou her sen - - tence!
Tenore.
Basso. Give thou her sen - - tence! Give thou her
poco a poco cresc.

Be.
honor shaken. Her ruin wrought,
W.
its slumber imbuing with eager
Sopr.
Give thou her sentence! Give thou her sentence!
Alto.
Give thou her sentence!
Ten.
sentence! Give thou her sentence!
Basso.
Give thou her sentence! Give thou her
poco a poco cresc.
Be.
defiant unbending.
W.
breath. Let mercy be
Give thou her sentence!
Give thou her sentence! Give thou her
Give thou her sentence!
sentence! Give thou her sentence!
21181

Bc.
She will not speak.
Then I
W.
ours her life re-new-ing,
her
Give thou her sen-tence swift unto death!
sen-tence!
Death!
swift unto death!
Give thou her sen-tence!
Death!
swift unto death!
Death!
swift unto death!
ff
Bc.
dare not de-lay!
W.
life re-new-ing.
Givethouher sen-tence! To death!
Givethouher sen-tence! To death!
Givethouher sen-tence! To death!
Givethouher sen-tence! To death!
ff
21141

Hester.
All-mighty fath - er end thou this woe!
To death!
To death!
H.
What ev - er doom to me shall come,
To death!
To death!
H.
spare not my sin, but lay me low despised ac -
cresc. poco a poco

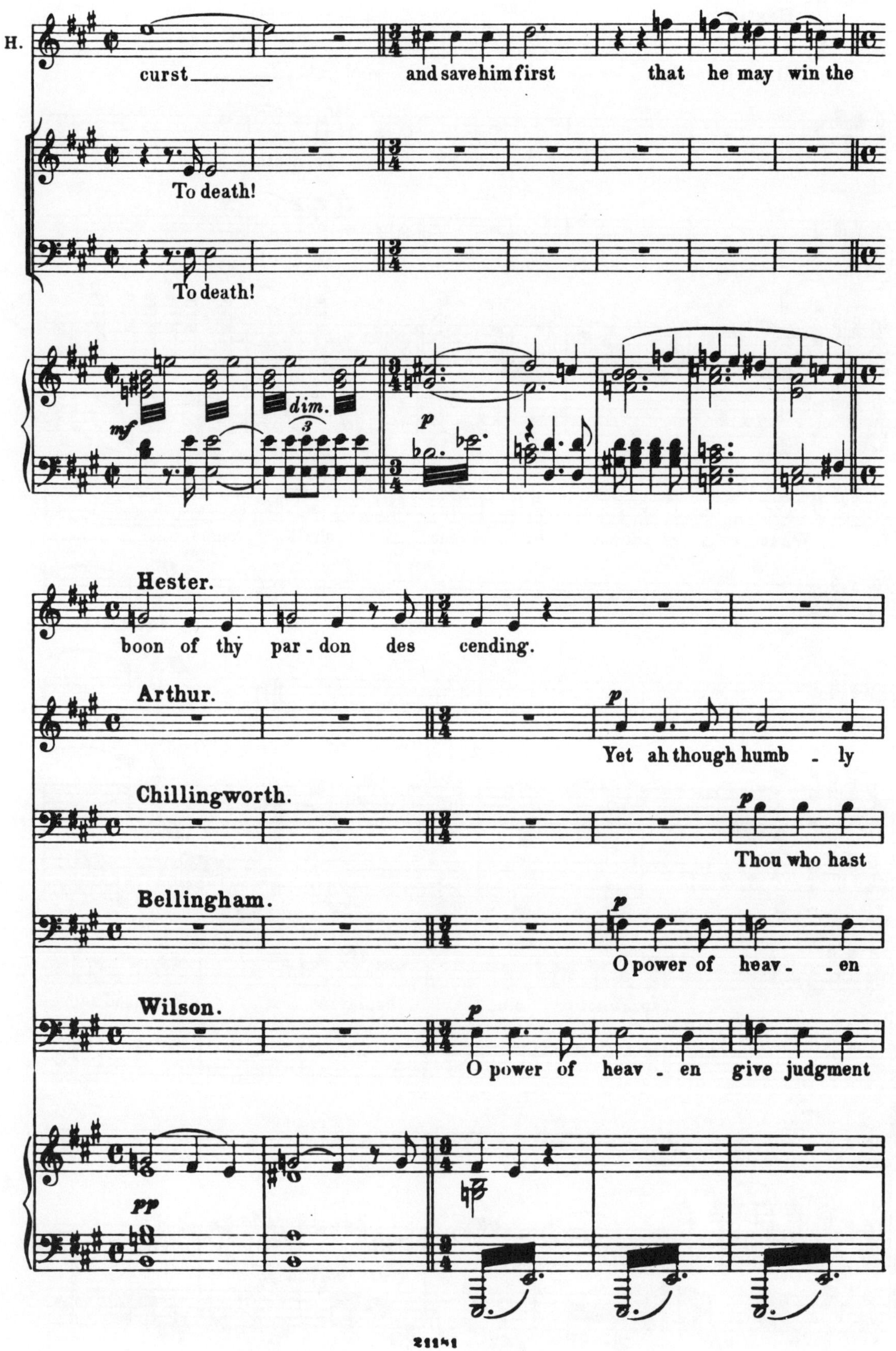
H.
curst
and save him first
that he may win the
To death!
To death!
mf
dim.
p
Hester.
boon of thy par - don des cending.
Arthur.
p
Yet ah though humb - ly
Chillingworth.
p
Thou who hast
Bellingham.
p
O power of heav - en
Wilson.
p
O power of heav - en give judgment
pp

A. I were to kneel, my guilt, my guilt to en - fold

C. brok - - en thy vows in dis - grace, may the Go - ver - nor spare thee

Be. give judgment wise to thy ser - vants here.

W. wise to thy ser - - - vants here.

Hearken, all hear - ken!

Hearken, all hear - ken!

A. all false-hood spurn - ing. Too

C. thee I would rule by the

Be. Hear - ken Lord, let your

W. Hear - ken Lord, let your

pp Hearken, all hear - ken!

pp Hearken, all hear - ken!

p

molto ritard.

ritard.
A.
late for her weal the truth would be told,
too
C.
p
shatt - ered heart
and truth for sworn
Be.
light on us rise,
your
W.
light on us rise,
your
f
What
may he de-clare!
f
What
may he de-clare!
ritard.
sf
pp
ritard.
A.
late for her weal the truth would be told,
for the
C.
mf
till I
en - snare thee
and make
thee
Be.
mf
glor - y
ap - pear,
your glor - y ap -
W.
mf
glor - y
ap - pear,
your glor - y ap -
p cresc. molto
What
may he declare?
our ru-ler un - daunted?
The
p cresc. molto
What
may he declare?
our ru-ler un - daunted?
The
cresc.
21141

Lento.
A.
flow'-ring dawn of her womanhood is lost in noon's hottest
C.
mourn thine ev - il part and his, poor fool, with
Be.
pear! In the words of the
W.
pear! In the words of the
doom in his face by com - pas - sion is haunted, would he grant her a grace and
doom in his face by com - pas - sion is haunted, would he grant her a grace and
Lento.
burn - ings.
doub - le woe con - tend - ing.
just.
just.
will he so dare, and will he so dare.
will he so dare, and will he so dare.

Andante.
A.
C.
Be.
W.
Would this tor - - ture were
All in vain her sil - ence!
Let your light on us rise and your glor -
Let your light on us rise and your glor - y ap -
p cresc.
Thy will be
Andante.
p
cresc. poco a poco
end - - - - ed!
- y ap - pear, O Lord!
pear, O Lord!
ff
dim. e ritard.
done, O Lord!
f

p
dim.
Thy will be done!
p
dim.
Thy will be done!
pp
8ve basso
Bellingham.
Hear, them! I de-cree not death.
f
Be.
Thou art free! But hence-forth a-part from oth-er folk
She is free?
She is free?
f
f
ff
p

Be.
she shall tar - ry, and there on thy heart thy life
pp
cresc.
Ped.
long carry the scar - - let
f
a tempo vivace
(Hester clutches at her bosom convulsively, and bows her head.)
let_ter!
The scar_let let - ter, and scar_let let - ter what
The scar_let let - ter, and scar_let let - ter what
The scar_let let - ter, the scar - let wo - man!
The scar_let let - ter, the scar - let wo - man!
a tempo vivace
f

re - tri - but - ion were bet - ter! Ha, ha, ha,
re - tri - but - ion were bet - ter! Ha, ha, ha,
What re - tri-but - ion were bet - ter!
What re - tri-but - ion were bet - ter!
ha, ha, ha, ha, ha, ha, ha, ha, ha, ha, ha, ha,
ha, ha, ha, ha, ha, ha, ha, ha, ha, ha, ha, ha,
Ha, ha, ha, ha, ha, ha, ha, ha, ha, ha, ha, ha, ha, ha, ha,
Ha, ha, ha, ha, ha, ha, ha, ha, ha, ha, ha, ha, ha, ha, ha,

all her life here - aft - er! Round her shall
all her life here - aft - er! Round her shall
all her life here - aft - er! Round her shall
all her life here - aft - er! Round her shall
Un poco più lento ma in tempo.
ring scorn and laught - - - - er!
ring scorn and laught - - - - er!
ring scorn and laught - - - - er!
ring scorn and laught - - - - er!
ff
dim.

(to Wilson)

Bell.

Now worthy Sir, for pray'r and

Be.

ser - mon pour on the mul - ti_tude the dew of

Be.

Her - mon thy balm_y e - loquence that in un - -

p

p

Be.

ion we dwell to - geth - - - er! Into the

cresc.

allargando

f

21161

(The Governor, Wilson and the others enter the Meeting House.)
Be.
church, good people, re - pair.
Andante grave.
pp
(As Arthur passes the Pillory his glance meets Hester's.
mf
He turns away with bowed head, his hand clutching his breast, while she remains standing erect and
mf
motionless on the Pillory.)
ff grandiosa
trem.
21151

(**Arthur** hurriedly, as if scourged by the knowledge of his guilt, enters the Meeting House.)

Un poco più allegro ed agitato.
8
ff
f

(The doors of the Meeting House close; only **Chillingworth** lingering near **Hester**, who begins to tremble violently.)

poco rallent.
pp
Hester.
My heart is broken. O shame and sor - row! Ah, how can I
f
mf
H.
bear the mor-row wear-ing this to - - ken.
(sinks down fainting)
f
Chill. (rushing up Pillory steps).
What has chanced here? She must not

Un poco più vivo.
C.
die. Now Ne-cro-mancy, come to my aid.
f
(He mixes a potion in a leathern cup, which with case bottles, he takes from his girdle; and pours
ff
the draught, within her lips.)
accel. e furioso
6
Più lento.
fp
sempre p
cresc. ed accel.

Più lento.

ff *dim.* *mp*

Hester (partly recovering).

To mine anguish leave me. I am not afraid to per-ish a-lone.

a tempo

f *f*

Chill.

Nay, look. It is I— dost thou not know— me?

Hester.

Thou! Thou?

Violente.

f *f*

H. Rog - - - - - - - er, of the darkling brow!

H. Whence ——— comest thou here?

Un poco più lento.

Chill. Hush, Hest - er have no fear! ———

C. —

Hester. But if thou know'st —

a tempo

f

21181

Chill.

rit.

Un poco largamente.

The worst I know!

R.H.

L.H.

rit.

Lento.

Chill.

Far ov_er o_cean stray - - ing, thee ______

C.
still tho' long de - lay - ing, I came to
find!
p
But lo! the un-faith - ful
sea wreck - ing us, cast me a -
cresc.

C.
shore
on a wild coast. Whence
wand'_ring long through the sil _ ent for _ est thee still to
find I came, till here
— in the mark - et place I be -

C. held thy face and thine op - en shame.

fp *ff*

Hester. (covering her face with her hands)

Oh! I can

dim.

H. bear no more. Will it bring me

Chillingworth.

Drink this, be strong!

(within the church)

CORO. Praise God from who

Praise God from who

p

21181

H.
death, then glad - ly shall I drink it to win re - lease.
all bless - - ings flow,
all bless - - ings flow,
R. H.
H.
Chillingworth.
No, it gives thee life and keeps thee liv - ing that so thine
praise
praise
fp
cresc. poco a poco
marcato

C.
in - famy's mark still may burn on thy bos - om.
him all creat -
him all creat -
Hester.
O pit - y - less thou and strange the charm thy pot - ion hath
ures here be - low.
ures here be - low.
fp
p
espress.
H.
wrought, as though all my thought were art - ful - ly lull'd by thy sooth - ing to
Praise him all ye
Praise him all ye
dim.
p
21181

Chillingworth.
H.
some dark spell.
Yea never to tell thy secret, save to
heav - en - ly hosts.
heav - en - ly hosts.
f
C.
me I ask not where-fore or how you fell.
Praise fath - - - er,
Praise fath - - - er,
p
fp
C.
Since from my birth de-formed, the
Son, and
Son, and
fp

espress.
C.
fault was mine to dream you loved me.
ho - - - - ly ghost.
ho - - - - ly ghost.
cresc.
sf
Hester.
Love I felt not nor feigned.
p
dim.
Allegro.
Chillingworth.
Yet thou hast wronged me, and the man is still
sf
p

C.
liv - ing who wronged us both! For him
there can be no for - giv - ing. Speak, Hester who
is he?
cresc. poco a poco
p
ff
Hester.
Allegro l'istesso tempo.
Nay ask me not,
dim.
mf

H.
no power can wring from me his name.
Chillingworth.
As in books I've sought truth and in Al - - chemy
C.
gold. Him I'll hunt — with-out ruth
p agitato
C.
till his se - - cret I hold.
p
f

Hester.
And then, thou wouldst kill?
f
Chillingworth.
Nay, let the man
Un poco più tranquillo ma in tempo.
p
C.
live, I o - bey heav - ens will.
a tempo
3
3
dolce
a tempo
p
Hester.
If its merc - y should give

H.
that in hon - - or he bide?
Chill.
Like a
cresc.
f
L'istesso tempo.
C.
star let him shine yet where - ev - - - - er he
f
p
C.
bide, he is
mf
C.
mine,
p
mf

C.
he is mine!
Hester.
Thy deeds feign merc_y but thy words are ter_ _ror.
L'istesso tempo.
Chill.
Thou'st kept the
C.
myst_e_ry of thy pa_ra_mour one thing I ask: that

C.
thou keep al - so mine.
None know me in this land
yet here's my home near thee,
near
p
f
mf
dim.
Molto più lento.
him.
But thou
be - tray me not!
pp
Hester.
Why dost thou lay up - on me this com -

Un poco più lento.
H.
mand?
Chill.
The husband to the world, as in one dead hence_forth the
Un poco più lento.
p
mf
Un poco più vivo.
C.
name of Chillingworth I bear. Thou re_cog_nize me not
cresc.
fp
mf
C.
by word or sign, nor breathe our se - cret to the man thou knowst; for
cresc.
dim.
p
C.
if thou dost, his fame his life will be
cresc.

C.
mine to des - troy. Hest - - er,
p misterioso e tranquillo
be - ware, be - ware!
p
Hester.
I will be se - cret for thee, for
dolce
Andante con moto.
H.
him.
Chill.
Ay, dwell in dark - ness ev - - er!
Andante con moto.
p un poco marcato

Hester.
How strange thy smile! O, art thou like the Blackman of the for-est,
cresc.
H.
hast thou en-tired my soul in-to a bond of ru-in.
mf
f
Chill.
rit.
Thy soul Hest-er, no, not thine!
rit.
Un poco più lento.
(within church)
CORO.
ff
God's voice breaks ce-dars,
ff
God's voice breaks ce-dars,
Un poco più lento.
ff

yea, God breaks Ce-dars of Le - ba - non.
yea, God breaks Ce-dars of Le - ba - non.

(Tumult and cries heard within church. The people troop forth in confusion, with **Bellingham** etc. Some of them carry **Arthur** in their arms.)

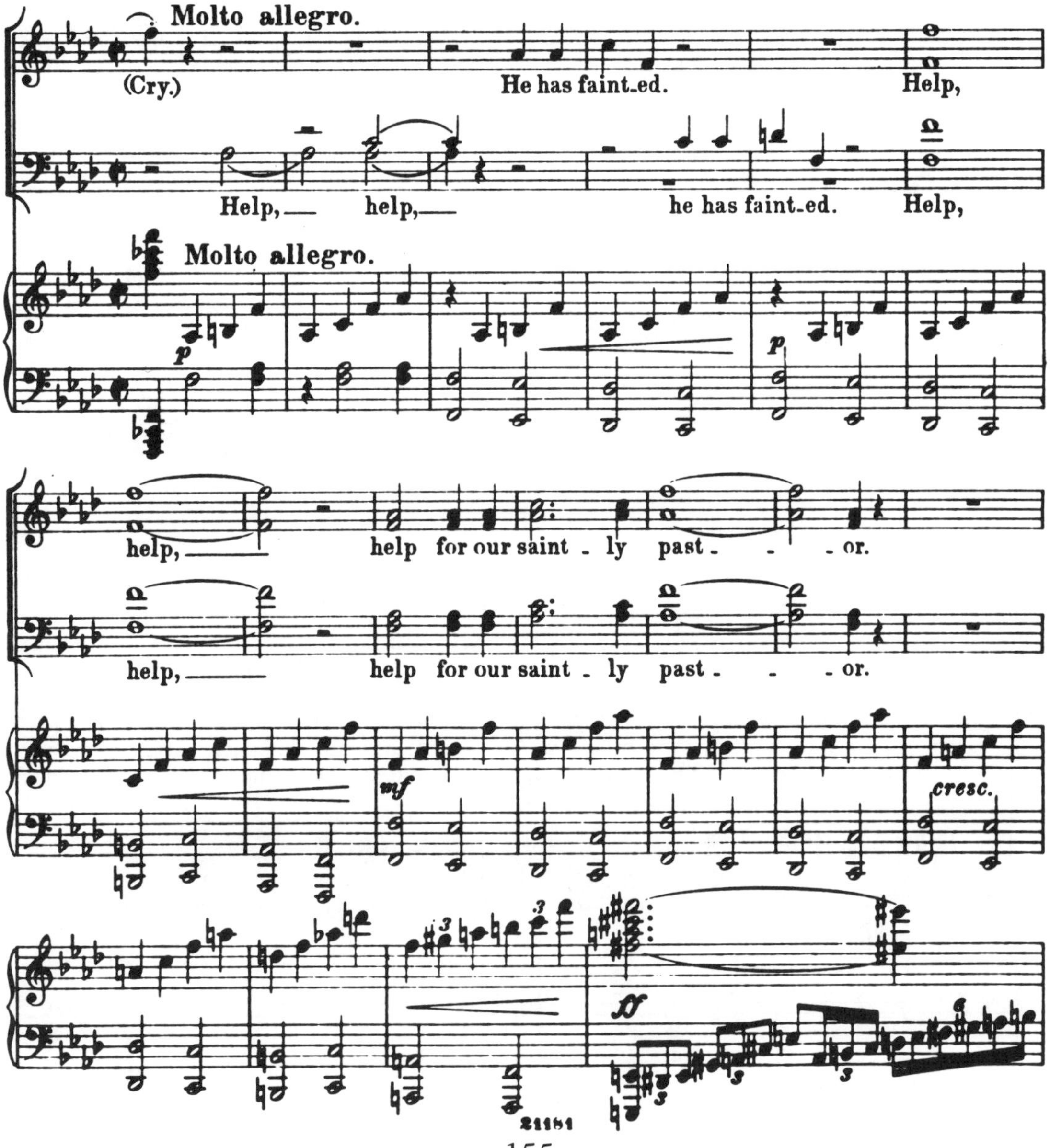

Molto allegro.

(Cry.) He has faint-ed. Help,

Help, help, he has faint-ed. Help,

Molto allegro.

p

help, help for our saint - ly past - - or.

help, help for our saint - ly past - - or.

mf *cresc.*

ff

21181

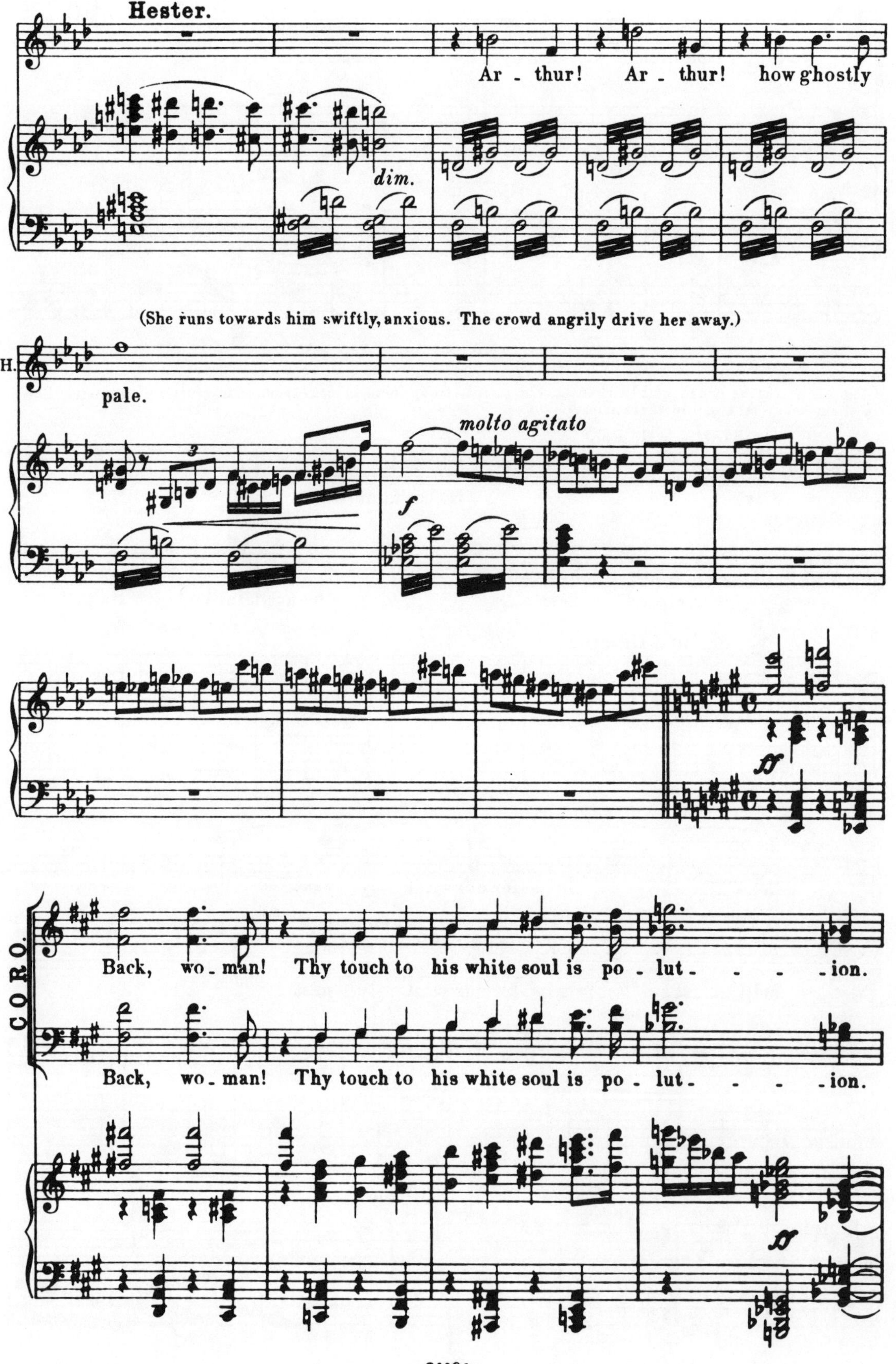
Hester.
Ar - thur! Ar - thur! how ghostly
dim.
(She runs towards him swiftly, anxious. The crowd angrily drive her away.)
H.
pale.
molto agitato
f
ff
CORO.
Back, wo - man! Thy touch to his white soul is po - lut - - - - ion.
Back, wo - man! Thy touch to his white soul is po - lut - - - - ion.
ff

Chill.
'Tis he, 'tis he! O won-der of
fp
C.
dark- -ness! I have found
fp
un poco rit.
sf sf
C.
the man.
sf sf
ff a tempo, furioso
rit.

Second Act.

Prelude.

(Curtain rises.) (The forest. Hester's Hut on one side. At back an opening among the trees, showing a forest path lost in obscurity. Sunlight alternates with deep shadow.

Indications of a brook among the trees; the light sparkling on it fitfully.)

H.

trees. Rest - less am I as the wat - ers

H.

mur - mur and wand - er - ing breeze.

R. H.

H.

Sunlight flies from me ere I near it; the brook's moan

mf

dim.

H.

stays. Grief nev - er dies from me: still I hear it through

mf

cresc

f

H
nights and days sob 'mid the wood - land, — the
H.
stream in - ton - ing my heart's own
dim.
H.
woe.
dim.
p
H.
Ah, sad brook - let why still art

H.

pp

moan - - ing? what dost thou know?

pp misterioso

pp *mp*

H.

Is it a se - - - cret of

H.

this dark for - - - est Told un - to

H.

thee; Fear - - some - ly wrong,

poco a poco cresc. e più agitato

H
that thou ab - horr - - est, and so must
flee.
Tempo primo subito.
ff
dim. ed rit.
Whispering ev - er the hapless
tid - ings? Couldst thou but cease; hushing thy plaint, with my spirits
p
pp
con espressione
fp
cresc.

(She sinks down upon a mossy bank by the brook, musing.)
H.
chi - - dings; I should find peace!
L.H.
un poco marcato
poco a poco dim.
dolce
Ah
still how gent - - - ly,
con espress.

H.
Blend - - - ing, re - turn - - ing with
long end - eav - - - or
5
un poco marc.
Fleet - ing as foam yet en -
dur - - ing for - ev - - - - - er
cresc.

Allegretto.
H.
Sweet thoughts of home a-
p
wake in me yearn - - - - ing!
cresc.
mf
and still my heart doth wand - - - er far to its
R.H.
L.H.
dim.
p
appassionato
child hood blest in dear old Eng - - land
pp
espress.
cresc. ed accel.
L.H.

H.
yond - - - er.
H.
Oh, in - - no-cence! flown like a bird
H.
from the storm-blown nest
cresc.
con molto espressione
H.
Come back to me!
fp
f
8

H.
Come back to me!
8
fp
f
Molto appassionato.
Dreams
sf
of the church - bell, and pray'rs that I
p
knew. Come true, come
dim.
rit.
rit.
rit.
rit.

(She kneels.)
Andante tranquillo.
H.
true!
L.H.
p
dim.
semplice e mezza voce
O Father of heav'n! if still to call thee
pp
p
father I dare:_
Grant me to do thy
will; my burden here to bear!
Un_to my heart re_

H.
store sweet faith a-gain, and rest, That hum-bly I once more may
H.
trust me to thy care.
pp
R.H.
Tranquillo.
mf con espressione
tranquillo
p
Ped.
mf
tranquillo
p
Ped.

mf un poco agitato

f

dim. poco a poco

R. H.

Ped.

un poco marc.

Ped.

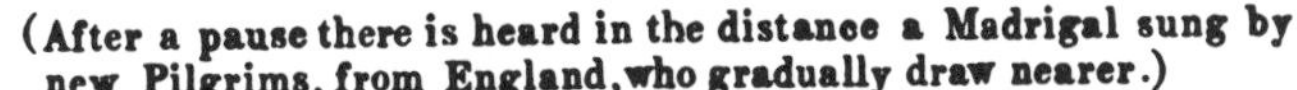
(After a pause there is heard in the distance a Madrigal sung by new Pilgrims, from England, who gradually draw nearer.)

Chorus of English Pilgrims. (behind the scenes)

hearts, our hearts to de_light, our hearts ——— to de_light our hearts to de_

hearts, our hearts to de_light, our_hearts, our hearts to de_

win our hearts, win our hearts to delight, our hearts to de_

light, our hearts ——— to de_light, win our hearts to de_

light. Who'd then at home be stay_ing, Who'd then at

light. Who'd then at home, at home be stay_ing, Who'd then at home, at

light. Who'd then at home be stay_ing, at home be stay_ing, Who'd at

light. Who'd then at home, at — home be stay_ing, Who'd then at

home be stay - ing. Up! Cast a_way dull sorrows weeds.

home be stay - ing. Up!

home be stay - ing. Up! Cast a_way dull

home, at home be stay_ing. Up! Cast a

Cast a - way, cast a - way dull
Up, cast a - way dull sor - rows weeds, cast a - way dull sor - rows
sor - rows weeds, cast a - way dull sor - rows weeds, dull sor - rows
way dull sor - rows weeds, Up, cast a - way dull sor - rows
sor - rows weeds, 'Tis time we go a - may - ing, 'tis time we go a - may -
weeds, 'Tis time, 'tis time we go a - may - ing, 'tis time we go a - may -
weeds, 'Tis time, 'tis time we go a - may - ing, 'tis time we go a - may -
weeds, 'Tis time we go a - may - ing, 'tis time we go a - may -
ing! Fal - leri, fallera, falleral - la - la, falle - ri, fallera, fallerallа -
ing! Fal - leri, fallera, falleral - la - la, falle - ri, fallera, falleralla -
ing! La la la la la la la la la la
ing! La la la la la la la la la la la la la la la la la la la la

pp mf

la — la — la — la — la la la la la! To the daisy's

pp mf

la — la — la — la — la la la la la! To the daisy's

pp mf

la la la la la la la la la! To the daisy's

pp

la la la la la la la la la la la la la!

breast the larks a-bove us, the larks a-bove, a-bove — us,

breast the larks, the larks a-bove us, a-bove — us, Rain —

breast the larks, — the larks, — the larks a-bove, Rain down

To the daisy's breast, Rain down heav'n's

cresc.

Rain down, rain down heav-en's song! "O listen and love, listen and

cresc.

— down heav-en's song, heav'n's song! "O list-en and

cresc.

heaven's song, rain down heav-en's song! "O listen, listen and love

cresc.

song, rain down heav-en's — song! "List-en and

f
love us, list - en and love us, — list - - - - en and love ——
f
love — us, ———— O list - en and love us, and love
f
us, O list - - en and love, ———— and love ——
f
love us, list - - - - en and love us, and love ——

dolce
us." And all the day long a -
dolce
us." And all the day long, a - mong, a -
dolce
us." And all the day long — a - mong the
dolce
us." And all the day long, all the day long a - mong the

p *cresc.*
mong the dais - ies playing, We re - member their strain, we re - member their strain, a
p *cresc.*
mong the dais - ies playing, We re - member their strain, we re - member their strain, a
p *cresc.*
dais - - ies — playing, We re - member their strain, we re - member their strain, a
p *cresc.*
dais - - ies — playing, We re - member their strain, we re - member their strain, a

cresc.
dream of the blest For so we go a-maying, for so we go a-maying! Falle-ri, falle-ra, falleral-la-la, falle-ri, falle-ra, falleral-la-
ing! La la la la la la la la la la
ing! La la la la la la la la la la la la la la la la la la la
la la la la la la la la la!
Andante con moto.

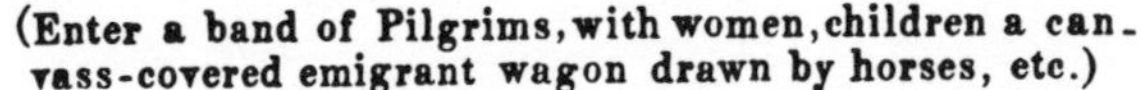
(Enter a band of Pilgrims, with women, children a canvass-covered emigrant wagon drawn by horses, etc.)

cresc. poco a poco

mf cresc.

f

(Hester advances, hesitating, towards the group, as though to welcome them.)

f

ff

Two Puritan men.
Nay, hold her a-loof, a witch is she and wanton too.
sfp
sfp
f
An outcast soul! Be-ware!
ff
rit.

(The Pilgrims draw away from **Hester** in dread and scorn. **Hester** suddenly remembering, shrinks, clutching the Scarlet Letter. The others continue to move away.)

pp
p
cresc.
Hester (alone).
Allegro.
O Rul - er of
f
ff
sfp
H.
Heav'n
are these thy
fp
6
p
creat - - - ures
can it
p
f

H.
be
Thou
hast
giv'n
to
men
thy
feat - - - ures,
with
hearts
of
clay
and
lips
of
fp
f
p
f
p

H.
flame
to black - en thy
sfp
im - age
a soul
to blast
in Thy
p L.H.
p
cresc.
name.
f un poco rit.
Ah,
then
fare - well
to meek re.
ff
p
f

H.

pent-ence: no long-er I dwell ___

H.

— in mer - cy's bound.

fp

H.

Lord give them sent - - - -

mf espressivo

H.

ence of an - - - - guish pro

H. found. As I, too, fling them my

H. curse like a brand from the fire of my

H. bos - - - - om.

H. May it burn and

with - - - - - - - er their
H.
wand - - - ering souls
H.
Hith - - - - er and thith - - - - -
H.
er cling to them

H.
haunt - - - - - - - ing, and hum -
p
H.
- ble their vaunt - - - - - - ing
p
H.
and crum - - ble in ash - - - - - -
p
6
H.
- - - - - - - - - - - - - es
R.H.
cresc.
L.H.

of end - - less
Un poco più lento.
(Goes into her hut, with a gesture of despair.)
(The scene darkens, as though with a passing cloud.)
H.
death!
espress.
perdendosi e rit.
(Enter Chillingworth and Gov. Bellingham.)
Bell.
Andante. Chill.
What cry was that? The wild wood

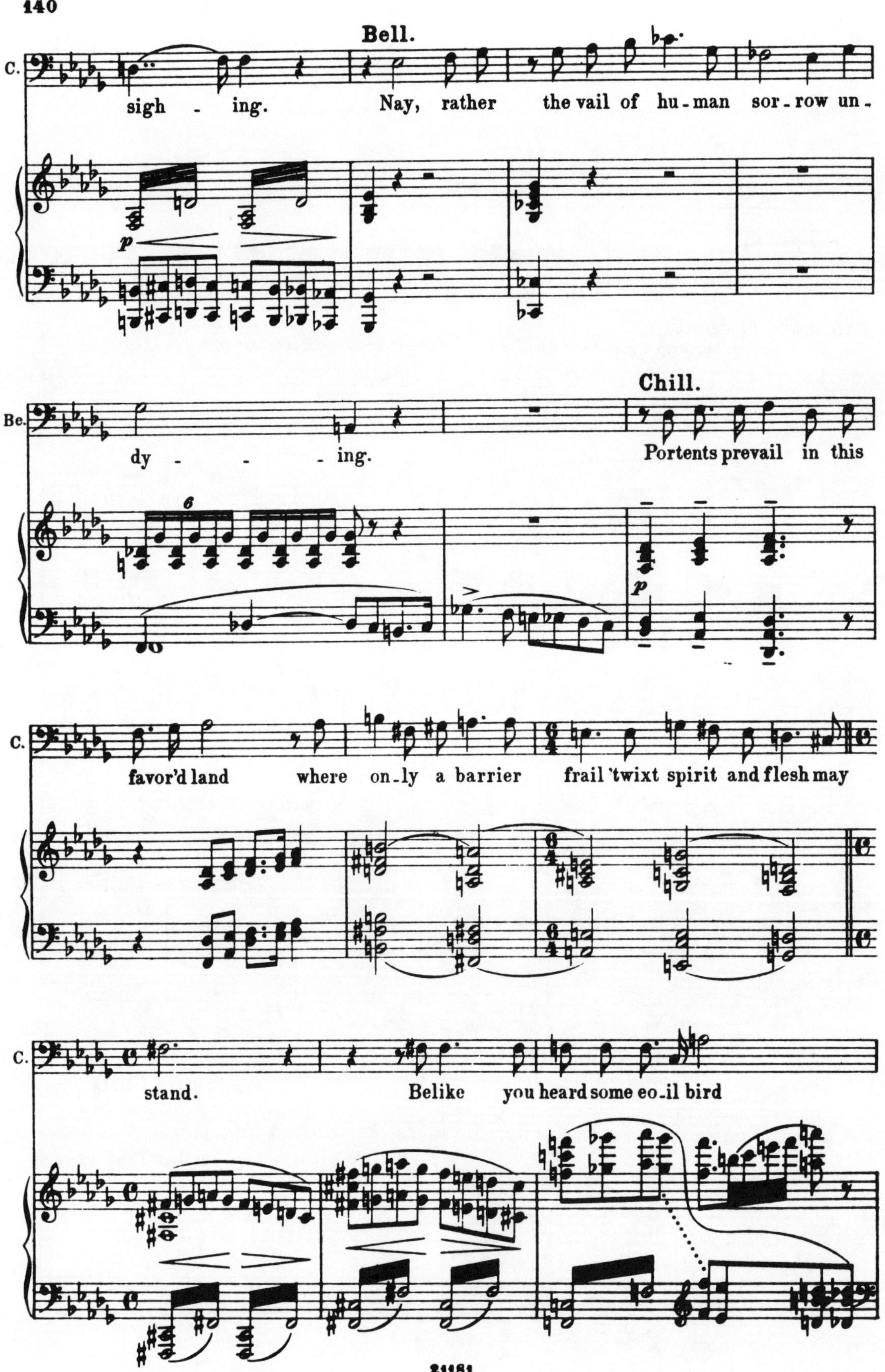
Bell.
C.
sigh - ing. Nay, rather the vail of hu-man sor-row un-
p
Chill.
Be.
dy - - - ing. Portents prevail in this
p
C.
favor'd land where on-ly a barrier frail 'twixt spirit and flesh may
C.
stand. Belike you heard some eo-il bird

C.
or the shriek of a dark soul wing - ing its
L.H.
f
dim.
Bell.
C.
way to the neth - er world.
Most lear - ned
pp
p
Be.
leech, thou art so skilled in nat - ure-speech with mar - vel filled
espr.
Be.
Tell me, canst thou yet reach the source of wast - ed
21181

Be.
woe that with ag - o-ny slow con-
cresc.
Be.
sumes the life of Ar - thur my friend?
Chill.
A strife without
cresc.
f
p
C.
end the an-cient myst-e-ry of bod-y and mind-
fp
C.
hid-den and strange the hist-o-ry!
Bell.
Much do I
p
p

Bc.
fear so great his worth so tend - er his spi - rit and pure
R.H.
Bc.
not long he will en - dure these bonds of earth
cresc.
Bc.
but leav - ing us lone - ly take flight to
p
un poco riten.
Chill.
heav'n. To heav'n? No, no! Of such dis - as - ter, be
un poco riten.
f

C. sure their need be no dread. I would not

grieve thee with thoughts of woe. Ar - thur I guard as the

un poco riten.

f un poco riten.

night guardes a flower from the sun strong-rayed

p

L.H.

p

if the blossom shall flour - - ish or fail or fade!

Bell.

C. Not well may I know.

Thou know'st him

dim.

p

p

Be. dear to us, save him, oh save! keep him still near to us far from the

Vivo. Chill.

Deep with - in me I

Be. grave.

Vivo.

p

C. cher - - ish de - sire that he live

p

C.
and ere he should per - ish my soul to per-
marcato
(exit)
Bell.
dit - ion I'd give.
Thou lovest him well.
Chill. (alone).
Ay, in - deed with the love of Hell!
dim.
With such love here I a - wait the hol - y man.

C.
Why does he ling-er a-far so late? To yonder lone-ly
mission he fared of Elliot, our Indian A - postle.
Ha! Can it be he has fan - cied or dared_ my plans to e -
lude.
In
Allegro tempestuoso.

C.
vain were the plan! For his life is pur-
fp
sued by the sil - ent
L.H.
p
foot - fall, still, of my hate while round him is
cresc. poco a poco
wov - en the web of his fate
fp

C. and I ev - er near as leech and friend

C. have watched the quiv - er - ing wounds of his

L.H.

C. soul My skill a lone has

C. kept him whole that ov - er him so I might

fp *cresc.* *fp*

C.
gloat
un - to the end.
cresc.
dim. poco a poco
No
no, he shall not die
as

mus - ic his cries of pain ring sweet trough my

p

C. brain;

p *cresc.*

f

C. and I live by my joy in his a - - go-

p *fp* *fp*

C. ny.

C.
He shall have life,
fp
C.
long life of
C.
rest - - - - less days,
p
and
cresc.
C.
nights of end - - - - - - - less
cresc.
p
cresc. -

Piu allegro.
woe.
ff
dim. poco a poco
rit.

R.H.
Andante un poco ritenuto.
(Enter, from the forest: Arthur.)
pp
p
f
Arthur (startled).
What? Is it thou my kind phy_sic_ian?
p
sf
Chill.
Yea, Ar_thur, wait_ing for ev_en now me_thought thou wouldst re_
mf
Allegro.
C.
turn.
Allegro.
p
mf
mf

Andante.
Arthur.
Good friend, I feel thy kind - ly will, — yet sometimes,
espressivo
wear - y, the soul must wand - er still, with on - ly God for its
dim.
Chill.
goal. Yet in thy weak - ness 'tis best thou
lean on me, and yield with meek - ness; for a grief at the

C.
spir - it's core like smoul - dring flame, will
cresc. poco a poco
set its mark on the out - ward frame.
f
Wouldst have me heal thy bod - i - ly woe?
dim.
p
p
f
accel.
Lay op - - - en the dark, deep
cresc.
fp

troub - - le or wound in the soul
cresc.
C.
be - low.
Arthur.
To thee? no, no!
A.
Nor to an - y phy - sic - ian of earth!
espressivo

A.
For a soul's dis - ease to the heal - er of
cresc.
A.
souls I go since He, as Him it may
fp
A.
please can kill, can
espressivo
3
5
A.
cure.
p
3

espressivo
mf
But who art thou,
A.
with daring so sure thy - - self to thrust 'twixt the
cresc. poco a poco
suf - - fer-er's dearth and the
boun - ty sup-reme all wise of his God?
f
rit. appassinato

A.
Chill.
Nay, I but told you that, which I must.
dim.
Più vivo quasi allegro.
C.
Be pat - ient, and heed; thy
pp
C.
strength guard well E - lect - ion ser - mon to-morrow thou
mf
cresc.

C.
preach_est.
Thy mind must be calm
to
weigh what thou teach - est, and min - is - ter balm to thy rev - 'rent
tr
p
flock
who bow be - fore thee and tru - ly a-
f
dore thee, their shep - herd, their saint and
ritenuto
affettuoso

C.
shelt_er_ing rock.
a tempo
mf
p
Too well thy
dim.
tend - - - er pit - y I know
thy heart still
R.H.
fp
bleeds for an - oth - er's woe,
fp

C.
and is ev - er op-pressed
Molto più lento.
with the sor - row of her whose
espressivo
wrong is con-fessed.
Arthur.
Chill.
Ha! Thou meanest_ Hest-er
(Arthur, greatly agitated, seems about to remonstrate, or deny; but Chillingworth continues.)
Prynne.
Allegro agitato.
mf

C.
Nay, dare not pro.
test
thou
shalt not de_ny!
Tur - - moil of soul
above all
thou must dread

rit.
For it saps thy force,
and deepens dis-
ff rit.
Andante.
C.
ease.
So good I know thee
p
so saint_ly
kind,
for this poor
wo_man
espress.
un poco rit.
thou
hast
re-
-pined.
(drily)
And so have I!
un poco rit.
dolce p

C.
But now, in_stead, calm thy com_passion! Canst not ap_pease her con_
p
_cience with thy sym _ _ _ _ _ _ _pathy?
(indicating Hester's hut)
f
L.H.
Lo, here she dwells: and now we are
espressione
p
p
nigh, wilt thou not see_ her?
Arthur (excited, amazed).
I? thou forgetest_
p
Ped.
Ped.

A.
how may it be, since here, condemned, she dwells a - part?
Chill.
Thou art her
C.
past - or. Thou hast the right to see her,
talk with her heart to
rit. molto
dim. e rit. molto

a tempo
Arthur.
C.
heart!
Dost thou think, that
a tempo
dolce
Chill.
A.
I, then—
Yea,
thou of
poco a poco più lento
C.
all
men:
Thy
heart is so
poco a poco più lento dim.
C.
pure.
Ah,
go to her,
go — to
R.H.
espressivo

Largo.
Arthur.
Chill.
her!
And thou, dost thou wait near?
Nay, homeward I fare: these
con espr.
Arthur (gives token of relief; aside).
herbs I now must dis_till.
At last, at last!
cresc.
Chill. (aside).
Now let her deal with the man as — she
will,
and the black flow_er

C.
blos - som as it may!
f Pesante.
Arthur.
For a time, fare - well!
Chill.
(aside)
(exit)
I go. Fare ill!
fp
f
f
dim
p

Arthur.

(alone)

espressivo

So long it seems— long years! I have dwelt a-mid darkness and tears, in the bonds of sin:— while ev-il has gnawed— at my life,— with-

out. And re - morse — has drained it, with.
A.
in.
A.
And long, ah, long — since I knew the touch — of a
A.
hap - - piness true and words without fear! Would
mf
dim.
pp
p
più f

A.

God I might break the chains of doubt,

f appassionato

A.

and call to thee, Hest - - -

ff

fp

pesante

A.

- - - er! Hest - - - - er! Hest - er!

mf

f

pp

(Turns away; sinking down on the moss.)

(Enter Hester, from hut.)

pp

p

R.H.

dim. perdendosi ppp

Hester.
Thou Arthur, here? 'tis I.
Arthur.
Who speaks? Thou, tru_ly,
p
pp
A.
Hest_er, here in life?
pp
pesante
Hester.
Molto più vivo.
Know'st thou me not? So long the time_'twixt then and now?
p
espressivo
molto cresc.
f
ff

Arthur.
rit.
I know thee well, but long the time 'twixt then and
rit. e dim.
pp
A.
now, for grief sets age up-on my
rit.
p rit.
Più lento.
A.
brow.
Pesante e più lento.
f
dim.
A.
But thou, ah, thou, hast thou found
p
p dolce

Hester (pausing, shakes head and makes a gesture).
Al - as! Or thou re-
A.
peace?
mf
Allegro. Arthur.
H.
lease? Nay, nought but des - pair! What else could be
fp
f
fp
A.
mine, since, tho' I wand - er with - er - so - e'er, my
f
fp
A.
life is wrapt in dark de - ceit.
fp
ff

21181

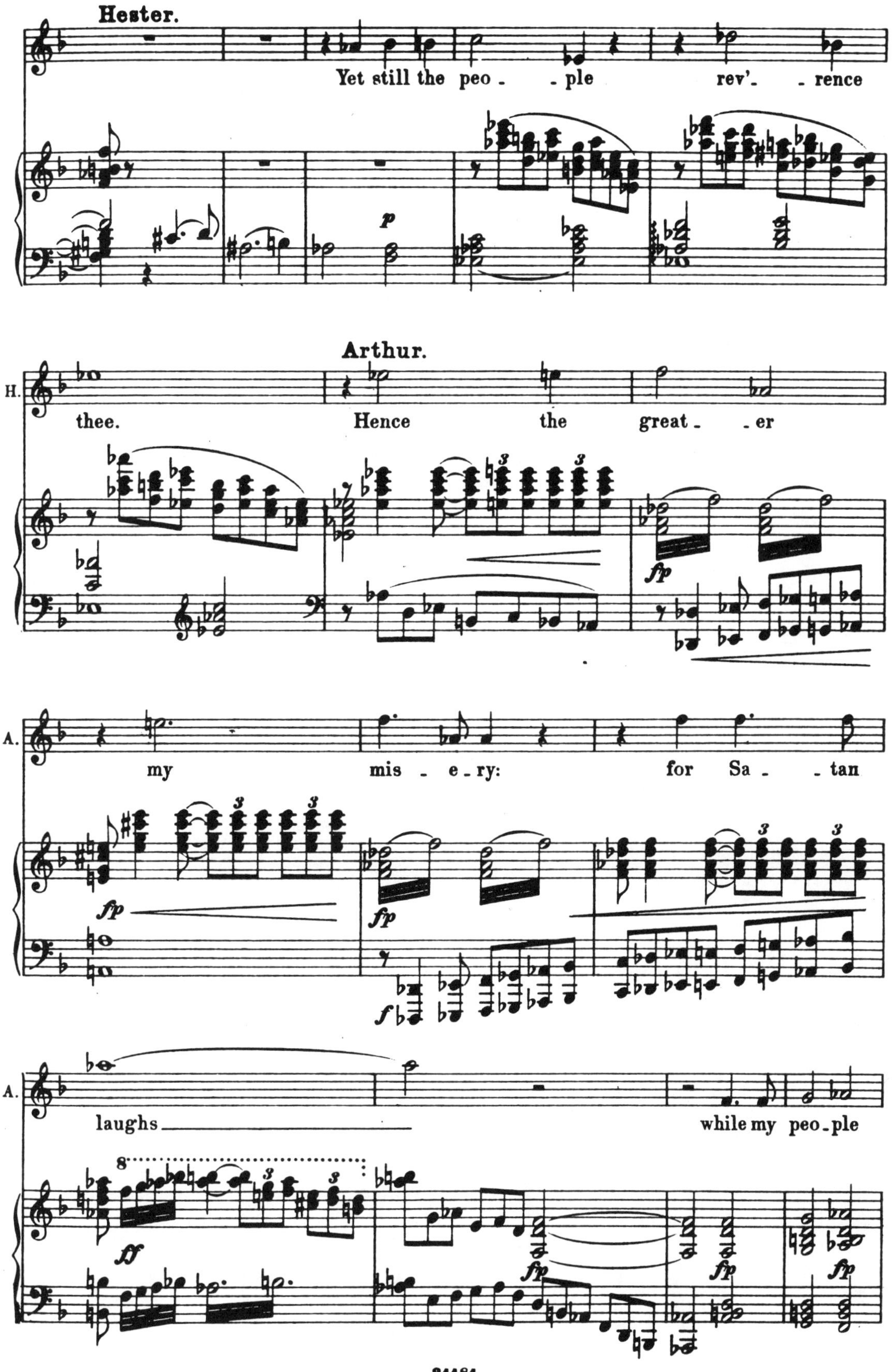
Hester.
Yet still the peo - ple rev' - rence
H.
thee.
Arthur.
Hence the great - er
A.
my mis - e - ry: for Sa - tan
A.
laughs while my peo - ple

A.
praise.
f
L.H.
f
3
3
Più lento.
A.
Hap - - py art thou, who
fp
5
f
Hester.
Hap - py!
A.
bear - est on thy breast the scar - let let - - ter!
ff
fp

H.
What dost thou say?
A.
Ay, better, far better to wear that raiment,
than life - - long lurk in despair. Woe unto
me! My letter in secret
still does burn with a flame that
f
p
espress.

A.
nev - - er, nev - - er dies as
cresc. poco a poco
tho' I stood at the judg - ment seat nor of - fer'd
ev - en con - fess - - - - - ions pay - ment
While
f

A.
rit.
_from the throne a _ bove like trum_pet_blasts___ I hear the accusing
3
rit.
Andante maestoso.
A.
voice:______ "Thou con_secarte and placed o'er men,
ff
ff
A.
to teach them pur - i - ty,
3
3
f
A.
false art thou to thy trust! thy call _ ing

A.
thou hast disgraced
Soiled are thy
robes, and thou li_est low in the
dust, a with_er'd bough, that God in_to
ritard.
Lento.
flame un_end_ing casts."
mf
fp
f
ritard.
mf
p

A.
Had I but one friend or a foe, the worst, be-
espress.
fore whom I might bend each day and be known as a sinner
vile E'en so much truth might re- - - concile my soul to
rit.
life.
dim.

Hester.
Such a friend thou hast, be - hold, in
H
me. O'er the bit - ter pres - - ent
H.
the vanished past of thy sin and mine, to weep
H.
with thee!
p
p
L.H.

Arthur.
Ay, friend so true for - giv - ing and tend - - er
could cha - ri - ty hu - - man, the wrong un - do
then were I saved by the faith of a woman thro' pit - y - ing
tears of rain - - - - - bow splend - - - or.
A.
fp
cresc.
f
espress.
p
tr
L.H

Hester.
Allegro.
A_las, not on_ly a
H.
friend serves thy be_half there dwells with
p
H.
thee un_der thy roof the en_ _ _
poco a poco cresc.
H.
_ _ _ e_my thou dost de_sire
agitato
f
f
21181

H.
a foe ac-curs - - - - -ed.
Arthur.
What meanst thou?
A.
That man;- Gray Chill-ingworth thou sayest that he
A.
-my soul's -deep may scan?
ff
mf
f
f

A.
But, since thou dost know,
Tell me:-
why is he my foe?
Hester.
Know then
H.
the truth
till now from thee
hid:
H.
This man of
dread who now
doth
f
p
fp
mf
f
f
p

H.
hold us both ap - palled
p
f
f
dim. e rit.
(Arthur staggers backward covering his
H.
was my husband.
a tempo
face with his hands.)
ff fierce
ff
R.H.
R.H.
Arthur.
Thy hus - - - band?
O hid - eous
fp

A.
thought, beyond be - lief!
Wo - man, what
A.
wrong hast thou done, my soul to lay bare with its an - guish of sin that
A.
he, like a hawk of the air
might pierce with
f
A.
in and the se - - cret black from my
fp
f
L.H.

A.
bos - -som tear?
R.H.
espressivo
p
A.
Where
A.
now shall I turn,- by mine en - -e-my
A.
pent? No re - fuge, now, for my
dim. poco a poco

A.
soul's distress. Save the tan - - - gle
A.
deep of the wil - derness
dim.
A.
where - in to
rit.
rit.
pp
Più lento.
A.
hide. Or else -
p

(Takes out a phial from within his vestments.)
A.
Ah, see!
pp
perdendosi
Grave.
Hest - er here - - in I
p
poco a poco cresc.
hold the key to the pris_on_ing
earth.
poco a poco cresc.
R.H.
p

A.
Wide it would op - - - - - en the
f
p
gate to a life be_yond.
mf
R.H.
For cunn - ing_ly Chill_ingworth this
f
mf
pois - on dis_tilled from herbs that give

A.
death.
Who knows if
f
A.
God willed,–
or hell-born hate
that I the potion
f
A.
found.
'Tis mine
be it a foe or
R. H.
f
A.
friend
if its lips
touch mine, my
f
f

Hester (seizes the poison-phial from him).
Allegro agitato.
A.
woe will end. No, no. It is not thine!
fp
cresc. poco a poco
H.
If free - - dom
f
fp
come it shall be from my — lips, not
p
those of death, — that strike thee dumb. Why here a-
L'istesso tempo.
mf

H.

bide? Is the world — not wide?

Nay; bend thy steps towards the sea it bore thee hith - er and so a - gain may car - ry thee hence, and make thee

fp *espressivo* *espressivo*

p *cresc.*

H.
free.
p
cresc.
ff
dim. e rit.
Arthur.
Andante grave.
I can_not go, no strength have I to bat_tle
p
A.
lon - ger.. Far from thee to toil and strive_ new life to
p
espressivo

A.
win the endless pain of sin un - spok - en
cresc. poco a poco
Più vivo.
my steps would track, and fling me prone.
Tempo I.
Ah, think,- in distant
rit.
lands to wander; ex - iled a - lone to die.
rit.
P espressivo
p
pp

Hester.
p
Thou shalt not go a - lone!
p
cresc.
Arthur.
Più vivo.
Hester.
Hest - er!
With thee I go!
mf
H.
we look not back but
H.
forth with brave en - deav - - - - - or.

H.
To thee my strength I lend,
cresc.
mf
my arm will shel - ter thee, my love en -
Un poco più vivo.
fold thee. No si - - - - - - - ren of
Più vivo.
death from me can with - hold thee.
p
cresc.

L'istesso tempo.
H.
Let our hearts take wing - as here the
f
sym - bol of wrong I fling from my breast for
rit. molto
rit. molto
a tempo
(Tearing off the Scarlet Letter, she throws it far from her. The white hood, dropping
ev_er.
a tempo
ff
strepitoso
from her head, lets her hair fall loose.)
ff
Ped.

21181

dim.

p

dim. e rit.

perdendosi

pp

Andante espressivo.

Hester.

Strong are we and young: Ay; thou art so, my

mf

mf

H. friend and dost thou not still find in me the

p

H. beau - ty once so dear to thee?

Arthur.

O Hest - - -

p

fp

A.
- - er! The glow of thy love
my love of life re-news. Thy
con fuoco
blood beats warm: With thee I brave the
storm.
cresc. molto

Più lento.

ff *dim.* R.H.

A. At last we are free, the

espressivo *p*

A. cloud of sor - row fades far be - hind us and

A. nev - er the mists of the fu - - ture shall

21181

Hester.
A
blind us. Ay; the past is
p
dolce
H.
un poco accel.
gone! We look to the com - - ing
cresc. ed un poco accel.
H.
years; since grief is done with, and dawn makes joy of our
f
H.
mid - - - - night fears.
dim.
p

Arthur.
Thro' the
A.
for - - - - est
the
A.
sun - shine
breaks
A.
in a

208
A.
flood of ra - - - - - - - - - - - - - - - -diance rolled
and with - in us the
splendor a - wakes of hap - - - piness yet un - told.
p
espress.
cresc.
f
21181

A.

Ah, Hest - er, the gol - den

p 3 R.H. *pp* 3

A.

ray of hope — shines bright in thine eyes.

pp 3 3 *con fuoco f* *tr* *dim. molto*

Un poco vivo. (misterioso)

Hester.

Lo, the wings of a ship in the bay

pp 3 3

H.

wait but for the wind to a - rise and wait us, with

3 3 3

H. bles - - sings di - vine, far ——— from this land of

Arthur.

Quick let us haste from the

p

cresc.

H. death.— ...and lin - - gering sha - dows ——— of old - -

A. de-sert vaste, and lin - gering sha - dows of old - - en

con fuoco

f

H. - en sor - - row. To fol - low the

A. sor - - row To fol - low the star of a

H.
star of a gold - en mor - row. The white sail
A.
gold - - en mor - row.
p
p
3
H.
gleams with a light of dreams it beckons us
A.
...with a light of dreams it beckons us
p
3
Più vivo.
H.
on with gladdening hope. No more in
f
A.
on with gladdening hope.
Più vivo.
8
cresc.
appassionato

H.
anguish dark to grope. To a land of
A.
No_ more in an_guish dark to grope.___
p cresc. poco a poco
H.
new life the ship's prow speeds.
A.
To a land of new life the ship's prow
Più vivo.
A.
speeds.
Hester.
Nor o - mens
fp
H.
drear ______ in its flight it

H.
heeds for grief
Arthur.
Nor o-mens drear in its flight it
p
cresc. poco a poco
H.
is but foam in the
A.
heeds for grief is but foam
8
10
strepitoso
3
ff
H.
sharp keel's fur - - - row.
A
in the sharp keel's fur - - - row.

Vivo.
H.
A.
Quick then es - cape!
Quick then es - cape!
Vivo.
mf
f
Nor cast one
Nor cast one
glance at the storm - y
glance at the storm - y
rit.
rit.

Presto.
H.
past!
A.
past!
Presto.
ff al fine
8
Più vivo.

Third Act.

(The Market-Place, as in Act I, with view of harbor at back. A crowd of Puritan men and women, intermingled with men from forest settlements. Sailors interspersed among crowd. Chillingworth is seen at one side, conferring closely with the Bristol Shipmaster. A crowd of English Pilgrims, just arriving at the Market Place. During their song Chillingworth leaves the Shipmaster and disappears in the crowd.)

spray, we come to the seed-time sowing of
spray, we come to the seed-time sowing of
spray, we come to the seed-time sowing of
spray, we come to the seed-time sowing of
Mas-sa-chusetts Bay. Then ho, to the new world, greet-ing,
Mas-sa-chusetts Bay. Then ho, to the new world, greet-ing,
Mas-sa-chusetts Bay. Then ho, to the new world, greet - ing,
Mas-sa-chusetts Bay. Then ho, then ho, to the new

ho, to the new world, greet - ing, ho, to the new,
ho, to the new world, greet - ing, ho, to the
ho, to the new world, greet - ing, ho, ho, to the
world, to the new world, greet - ing, ho, ho,
L. H.
ho, to the new, ho, to the new world, greet - ing,
new world, ho, to the new world, greet - ing,
new, ho, to the new world, then ho,
ho, ho, ho, ho, to the new, ho, to the
L. H.

then ho,_ to the new world,greet - ing; and a hey for the
ho, to the new world,greet - ing; and a hey for the
ho,_ to the new world, greet - ing, greet - ing; and a hey for the
new world, to the new world,greet - ing,and a hey for the
Pilgrim, hey! and a hey for the Pil - grim, hey! and a
Pilgrim, hey! and a hey for the Pil - grim, hey! and a
Pilgrim, hey! and a hey for the Pil - grim, hey! and a
Pilgrim, hey! and a hey for the Pil - grim, hey! and a

21181

hey_ for the Pilgrim, hey! and a hey for the Pil - grim,
hey for the Pil - grim, hey! for the Pil - grim,
hey for the Pil - grim,and a hey_ for the Pil-grim, Pil - grim,
hey for the Pil - grim, hey for the Pil - grim,
hey!
With
mf
f

hope for the morrow and ev'- ry day; or
hope for the morrow and ev'- ry day; or
hope for the morrow and ev'- ry day; or
hope for the morrow and ev'- ry day; or
p
mf
mf
be it for gladness or sorrow, in New England we will
be it for gladness or sorrow, in New England we will
be it for gladness or sorrow, in New England we will
be it for gladness or sorrow, in New England we will

stay,— each true man with his sweet-ing, each
stay,— each true man with his sweet-ing, each
stay,— each true man with his
stay,— each true man with his
mf
10
true man with his sweet-ing,— and the law of the land, and the
true man with his sweet-ing,— and the law of the land, and the
sweet-ing, each true man with his sweet - ing,— and the
sweet-ing, each true man with his sweet - ing,— and the
più f
f risoluto

law of the land o - bey!
law of the land o - bey!
law of the land o - bey!
law_ of the land o - bey!
With a hey for the Pilgrim, hey! with a
With a hey for the Pilgrim, hey!
With a hey for the Pilgrim, hey!
With a hey for the Pilgrim, hey!

hey for the Pil-grim, hey! and a hey for the Pilgrim, hey! and a
and a hey for the Pilgrim, hey! and a hey for the Pil - grim,
and a hey for the Pilgrim, hey! and a hey for the Pil - grim, and a
and a hey for the Pilgrim, hey! and a hey for the Pil - grim,
hey! for the Pilgrim, hey!
hey! for the Pilgrim, hey!
hey for the Pilgrim, Pilgrim, hey!
hey! for the Pilgrim, hey!
21181

Shipmaster (crossing the stage).
But as for me_ to the an - cient is_land lies my
way. How_ev - - er wild the waves may
be._ I, in

sooth, my-self am wild; and yet, a faith-ful child,
S.
dear moth - er Eng - land I long, I
p
mf
cresc.
S.
long to see.
CORO.
With a hey for the Pilgrim, hey! with a
The new Pilgrims.
With a hey for the Pilgrim, hey!
With a hey for the Pilgrim, hey!
With a hey for the Pilgrim, hey!
f

hey for the Pil-grim, hey! and a hey for the Pilgrim, hey! and a
and a hey for the Pilgrim, hey! and a hey for the Pil-grim,
and a hey for the Pilgrim, hey! and a hey for the Pil-grim, and a
and a hey for the Pilgrim, hey! and a hey for the Pil-grim,
hey for the Pilgrim, hey!
hey! for the Pilgrim, hey!
hey for the Pilgrim, Pilgrim, hey!
hey! for the Pilgrim, hey!

Un poco più vivo, alla marcia.
(Chorus behind the scenes.)
Hark! they are com - ing in
Hark! they are com - ing in
Hark, hark! hark, they are
Hark, hark! hark, they are
Un poco più vivo, alla marcia.
(Music of Procession heard in distance. The crowd surges off
p
(Stage trumpets and drums gradually approaching.)
state - ly ar - ray. Hear the proud mus - ic, the
state - ly ar - ray. Hear the proud mus - ic, the
com - - ing in state - ly ar - ray. Hear the proud mus - ic, the
com - - ing in state - ly ar - ray. Hear the proud mus - ic, the
to one side, looking for the pageant to approach.)
cresc. poco a poco

roll of the drumming: Cheer, now, cheer for E - lect - ion Day! The
roll of the drumming: Cheer, now, cheer for E - lect - ion Day! The
roll of the drumming: Cheer, now, cheer for E - lect - ion Day! The
roll of the drumming: Cheer, now, cheer for E - lect - ion Day! The
f
(Orchestra.)
min - ister true and the new magistrate once more will ope to us
min - ister true and the new magistrate once more will ope to us
min - ister true and the new magistrate once more will ope to us
min - ister true and the new magistrate once more will ope to us

lib - erty's gate, and close it against all hard - y sin. Thank
lib - erty's gate, and close it against all hard - y sin. Thank
lib - erty's gate, and close it against all hard - y sin. Thank
lib - erty's gate, and close it against all hard - y sin. Thank
heav - en we stand the gate with - - in!
heav - en we stand the gate with - - in!
heav - en we stand the gate with - - in!
heav - en we stand the gate with - - in!
(Enter Hester.)
(Those of the people, who are nearest her, shrink away.)

Più vivo ed accel. poco a poco.
The sign of thy sin a mag - ic
The sign of thy sin a mag - ic
The sign of thy sin a mag - ic
The sign of thy sin a mag - ic
Più vivo ed accel. poco a poco.
cir - cle has drawn a - round thee; Scorn
cir - cle has drawn a - round thee; Scorn
cir - cle has drawn a - round thee; Scorn
cir - cle has drawn a - round thee; Scorn
ff

— ev - er shall hound thee! A-way! A-

— ev - er shall hound thee! A-way! A-

— ev - er shall hound thee! A-way! A-

— ev - er shall hound thee! A-way! A-

way! A - way!

way! A - way!

way! A - way!

way! A - way!

(They leave the stage.

dim. e rit.
p
Hester.
Più lento, quasi andante.
A - lone? ay, glad - - - -
ff
f
rit.
H.
- - - ly; for not, as once, an
dim.
p
espressivo

H.
out_cast prone I lie at your feet. My
free_dom I greet, and move a_part — no long_er sad - - - ly!
p
No long_er to you a bond - slave I moan, nor
p
espress.
dark spells — now my soul de_file. —
p
cresc.

H.
On the Scar_let Let_ _ter look your
f
3
fp
last!
fp
f
3
For, yet a litt_le while, your
Un poco più vivo.
ty_rant sway is past.
Tho' now I must
p
yield,
there in the for_est vast the
p
R. H.
poco a poco cresc.

H.
blight from my bos - som I cast:
If
here I en - dure it a - gain,
to tri - - umph is turned this
out - ward stain.—
Soon,

H
soon beyond your reach, harsh — peop - le mer - ci - less,
p
H.
I fly — to the whis - pering tide and the loved —
pp
H.
— one's ca - ress. Yon dark myst - er - ious sea
dol.
p
H.
più tranquillo
will hide my wrong — and my
PP rit. un poco
perdendosi
Ped.

a tempo
hap - piness from your ev - il speech!
a tempo
cresc.
L.H.
p
mf
H.
p
mf
H.
espressivo
cresc.
ff
(To the Shipmaster, who has come near her.)
H.
God greet thee! All is well?
Shipmaster.
Ay, mistress; if I dare
R.H.
f
p

S.
say so! I have it on truth of a witches word; and witches, I've heard,
mf
S.
know dark-ness from light. Our barque is ready:
fp
f mf
S.
at an-chor she rides for a turn of the tides: and, wind holding
f
S.
steady, we sail to-night.
f
mf

S.
Good om-en I deem it, and
p
S.
com-pa-ny rare, that you, sweet Lad - y, with us will
p
5
Hester.
S.
fare. Dost thou not know the best of omens
mf
dim.
p
H.
thou canst hope will be his presence who goes with me?
R.H.
tr
tr

Shipm.
Is it tru-ly so, then darkly I grope. Didst thou not say he
fp
p
tr
p
S.
flies in fear of hurt from the Pu-ri-tan Fath-ers here?
riten.
a tempo
If wrong he has wrought, how can his presence with
a tempo
fp
fp riten.
bles-sing be fraught? Still, the better, say I, if saint he
mf

Un poco ritenuto ma in tempo.
S.
be!
Since thou spokest, last_night, of
f
pas_sage flight,
yon old leech came to
p
seek a berth.
He, too, it seems, would cross the earth.
mf
cresc. poco a poco
If saint and doctor to_gether go,
fair winds in_deed must
f
f
tr
L.H.

Allegro agitato.
Hester (aside).
S.
blow.
Ah! worse than death those words pre -
fp
(to Shipmaster)
H.
sage!
You leech? What mean you?
f Primo tempo ritenuto.
p
Shipm.
Why, he — the old chi - rurgeon mage: know you
not? —
Allegro agitato.
Hester.
S.
Chill - ingworth. Then he, too, — has
accel.

H.
seen you? Dost tell me now that he will sail with
f
H.
us on your ship?
riten.
Pesante ma con spirito.
Shipm.
Ay; with a fav - oring gale and glad - some weath - er,
mf
S.
to these bitter folk we'll give the slip.

S.
Is it not well done? He,– the
S.
hump-shouldered one –
long has he
fp
S.
known your friend: They've dwelt to-geth-er. The
f
S.
leech will cling to him un-to the
p
un poco riten.

(He leaves her and mingles with the crowd.)

H.
lost!
Nor in this
a tempo
new
world
so - li - tude,
or a - mid sea tossed,
can we the black en -

Più lento.
H.
chant - ment e - lude!
ritardando
f
(She perceives Chillingworth at the opposite side of the market-place, smiling at her with vindic-
f
mf

tive meaning.)

Chill. (on opposite side of market-place).

C.
In
p
cresc.
Più lento.
Hester.
O dev - il-face and mock-ing smile!
C.
vain the wile of flight or turn - ing; and
Più lento.
p

H.
_ Where watchful mal - - ice ev - er lurks! _ What
C.
wast - - ed all her woe - ful cries! For
H.
ser - pent in that heart of guile ___ so som - bre dwells and
C.
un - to my hate, like in - - cense burn - ing,
p
H.
sly - - - - - - ly works, _
C.
her flame of a - go - ny doth rise. The
f

H.
our plot he un-rid-dles; our
C.
last word is spok - - - en; her last hope
p
f
p
Un poco più vivo.
H.
hope fore - stalls, with craft un-
C.
brok - - en; her with her lov - er hence
f
Un poco più vivo.
p
H.
known. Clos - - - er he
C.
forth I hold in the mesh of my
p

H.
holds us than pris - - - on -
C.
net. They shall rend - - er me
H.
walls:
Hate is
C.
yet a heav - ier price of their
H.
hard - - er than stone.
Ah, if un-to
C.
wrong, than gold.

H.
Arth_ur one word of warn_ing I might but speak!
C.
And what can their anguish weigh 'gainst the hurt to my hid - - den
H.
Yet, a - las, 'mid the mult - i_tude scorn - ing,
C.
pride? Or go they or stay, my ven - - - geance they
p
R.H.
H.
the sole one who loves me I dare not seek.
C.
still must a - bide, and in tort - ure burn; — for all en_

Help, help! Will God not find us,
treat-ing of pit - y I spurn.
cresc.
fp
'mid the snares of Hell that bind us?
p
p
mf
Più lento.
espressivo

dim. poco a poco

p

p perdendosi

(Stage Band from distance coming nearer and nearer.)
Drum.
Piccolo.

Coro.

(Behind the scenes.)

Soprano.
How gail - y they play! They

Alto.
How gail - y they play! They

Tenore.
How gail - y they play! They

Basso.
How gail - y they play! They

8

Cornets.

(Enter Band of musicians,

know the tune for E - lect - ion Day.

know the tune for E - lect - ion Day.

know the tune for E - lect - ion Day.

know the tune for E - lect - ion Day.

8

from one side, followed by the populace.)

(Enter escort of Citizen

21181

Soldiers — the Ancient and Honorable Artillery Company — in burnished steel, with gay plumes

Lo! — And the mag - - is - trates! — They come with

Lo! — And the mag - - is - trates! — They come with

— Lo! — And the mag - - is - trates! — They come with

— Lo! — And the mag - - is - trates! — They come with

nodding over their morions.)

(Enter Bellingham.)

fit - ting foot - steps slow. Thou

fit - ting foot - steps slow. Thou

fit - ting foot - steps slow. Thou, thou

fit - ting foot - steps slow. Thou, —

260
who wast gov - er - nor,— praised be thy
who wast gov - er - nor,— praised be thy
who wast gov - er - nor,— praised be thy skill, be thy
who wast gov - er - nor,— praised be thy skill, be thy

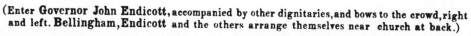

(Enter Governor John Endicott, accompanied by other dignitaries, and bows to the crowd, right and left. Bellingham, Endicott and the others arrange themselves near church at back.)

skill! But now we greet
skill! But now we greet
skill! But now we greet
skill! But now we greet
ff

our new rul - - er, the choice of the

our new rul - - er,

our new rul - - er, the choice of the peop - le's

our new rul - - er, the

peop - le's will, the choice of their will. Beat loud the

the choice of the peop - - - le's will. Beat loud the

will, the choice of the people's will.—— Beat loud the

choice of the peop - le's will, the peop-le's will. Beat loud the

drums! John En-di-cott comes. En-di-cott! En-di-cott!
drums! John En-di-cott comes. En-di-cott! En-di-cott!
drums! John En-di-cott comes. En-di-cott! En-di-cott!
drums! John En-di-cott comes. En-di-cott! En-di-cott!
Gov - - ernor e - lect!
Gov - - ernor e - lect!
Gov - - ernor e - lect!
Gov - - ernor e - lect!

L'istesso tempo.

p

Be - hold our

p

Be - hold our

p

Be - hold our

p

Be - hold our

L'istesso tempo. ♩ = ♩

mf

p

past - or— dear Mast - - er

past - or— dear Mast - - er

past - or— dear Mast - - er

past - or— dear Mast - - er

Arth - ur. And yet his face— how pale!
Arth - ur. And yet his face— how pale!
Arth - ur. And yet his face— how pale!
Arth - ur. And yet his face— how pale!
dim.
A shad - ow sab - le draws round him as he ad - vanc - es.
dim.
A shad - ow draws round him as he ad-
dim.
A shad - ow sab - le draws round him as he ad - vanc - es.
dim.
A shad - ow draws round him as he ad-
mf
dim.

cresc.
No, these are fanc - ies; for see how
vanc - es.
No, these are fanc - ies;
vanc - es.
No, these are fanc - ies;
cresc.
firm and e-rect he steps, as though some pur- -pose
...for see how firm he steps, as though some pur- -pose
...for see how firm he steps, as though some pur- -pose
for see how firm he steps, some pur- -pose
L.H.

high his weak - ness were sus - tain - - - ing.
high his weak - ness were sus - tain - - - ing.
high his weak - ness were sus - tain - - - ing.
high his weak - ness were sus - tain - - - ing.
cresc.
ff
God - giv - en im - pulse on - ly, past all fear,
God - giv - en im - pulse on - ly, past all fear,
God - giv - en im - pulse on - ly, past all fear, could guide his
God - giv - en im - pulse on - ly, past all fear, could

could guide his forc - es frail to bring us here his
his treas - ure of
forc - es frail to bring us here his treas - ure of
guide his forc - es frail to bring us
treas - ure of teach - ing, and bount - eous preach - ing-
teach - ing, and bount - e - ous preach - ing- sweet thoughts on us
sweet thoughts up -
teach - ing, and bount - e - ous preach - ing- sweet thoughts on us
here his bount - e - ous preach - ing- sweet thoughts up -

sweet thoughts up-on us rain - ing. Wel - come our
rain - ing, sweet thoughts up-on us rain - ing. Wel - come our
on us,
rain - ing, sweet thoughts up-on us rain - ing. Wel - come our
on us rain - ing. Hail! hail!
mf cresc.
past - or, our hope that can - not fail,
past - or, our hope that can - not fail,
past - or, our hope that can - not fail,
hail! hail!
dim. poco a poco

(Enter **Arthur** with **Wilson. Bellingham, Endicott** and the others wait for **Arthur** to approach the church, through the lane which they have formed. **Arthur**, standing erect, yet apparently weak physically, pauses.

Then, instead of going towards the church, he turns, crosses the stage slowly, and beckons to **Hester**.)

(Hester, who till now has remained where she was, half crouching in despair, draws herself up and moves towards him slowly, as if spell-bound.)

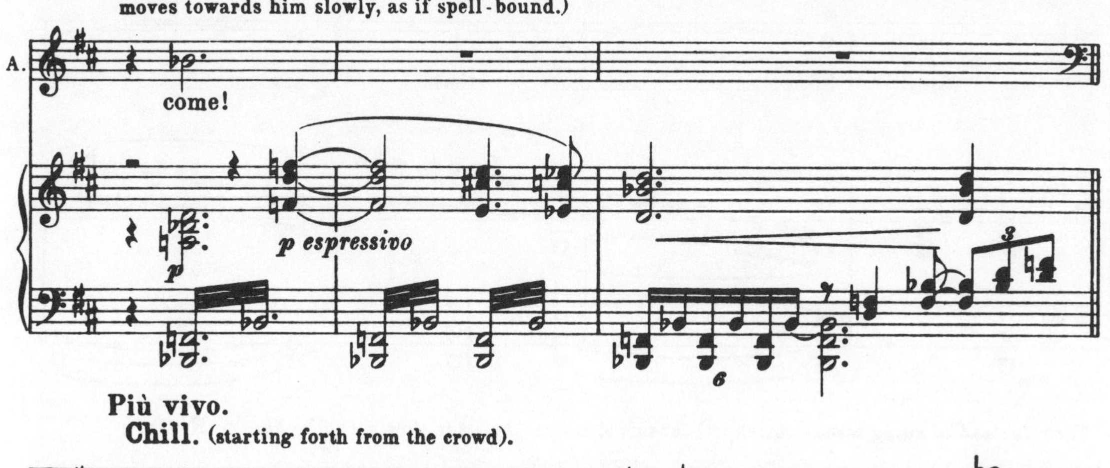

C.
I yet can save you: all shall be well.
Andante.
Arthur.
Ha, tempt - - er ap - pal - ling, thou art too
A.
late!
Thy pow - er no
A.
long - er my life con - trols:

A.
A spir - it strong - er than thine quells thy
p
A.
hate.
God is might - y a -
p
f
A.
bove us.
The soul of souls my will at last sets free
A.
from thine:
I shall es - cape thee
f
rit.

Allegro.
A.
now!
Soprano.
What trou_ble does Sat _ an for us de _ sign? Some
Alto.
What trou_ble does Sat _ an for us de _ sign? Some
CORO.
Tenore.
What trou_ble does Sat _ an for us de _ sign? Some
Basso.
What trou_ble does Sat _ an for us de _ sign? Some
Allegro.
mf
f
phan_ta_sy strange, pur _ su_ing the blame_less mind, his reas _ on has
phan_ta_sy strange, pur _ su_ing the blame_less mind, his reas _
phan_ta_sy strange, pur _ su_ing the blame_less mind, his reas _
phan_ta_sy strange, pur _ su_ing the blame_less mind, his reas _
f
ff

shak - en!
on has shak - en!
on has shak - en!
on has shak - en!
Molto più lento.
Arthur.
Come, Hest - er Prynne, thou who knowest my
dim.
p
A.
sin; Ay, Hest - er, come in His
un poco cresc.

name, so terr - - i - ble,
pp
A.
yet in mer - - - cy so mild, who has
grant - ed me grace at the fin - al hour to pro -
cresc.
Un poco più moto.
claim my wick - edness here, and face to face, the
p
espressivo
L. H.

A.
ev - il so long with-in be-moaned, but nev - er
f
A.
owned, a-loud to speak.
f
dim.
R.H.
p
rall.
L.H.
Andante con moto.
A.
Thy of - fered strength a - round me twine;
p

A.
but let it o - bey the will di - vine!
cresc.
mf dim. e rall.
A.
Ah, Hest - er, I
A.
need thee;
f
for
10
A.
stricken, wear - y and weak, now at the end, tho' it
mf
p
p

A.
be but with steps of a litt-le child,—
yon
rit. - - -
Lento.
(He points to the Pillory, taking Hester's hand.
scaf-fold with thee will I a - scend.
rit. - - -
Lento.
cresc.
f
ff
p
The people murmur, but are dazed, and dare not interpose, as Arthur and Hester move towards
p ma pesante
cresc.
the Pillory, and mount it. Chillingworth follows them to the steps.)
mf
cresc.
f
dim. poco a poco
mf
dim.

Più moto.

Wilson.

Arthur, Arthur, this magic forsake: to thy true self a - wake!

pp

L.H.

R.H.

p

Lento. **Arthur** (standing with **Hester** on Pillory).

Ye people of New England! ye still who

p

p

A. love me, and hol - y have deemed me! Your pastor be-

A. hold, not as you long have dreamed me,

p

fp

A.
but, as Heav'n shines high a_bove me,_
10
f
fp
so of all sin_ners the low_ _ _ _ _ _
6
11
_est, from falsehood's seed I garner disgrace:
espressivo
fp
p espressivo
3
But, lo, I up_ _root_ the shriveled weed,
cresc.
mf
cresc.

and the flow - - er of truth blooms
R.H.
Un poco più moto.
A.
here, in its place!
Agitato.
A.
The Scar-let Let - - ter

A.
that Hest - er wears — ye have shuddered at,
Poco a poco agitato.
long: But its lurid ray was but as a shad-ow of that fierce
cresc.
fire of smothered wrong that, night and day, with flam - - - - -
cresc.
- - ing despairs my breast has

scarred,
and
brand
A.
ed
my
soul!
Her fellow in
sin,
I have won my de - sire
and reached my
goal;
For
p
f
p cresc.
tr

Doppio movimento.

A.
I stand now be - side her, the
debt of my guilt's con - fess - ion to pay,
so long de - nied her.
If a - ny here
f
p rit.
f
Ped.

A. till God's — judgement de - ny,

p *p*

A. here now ere I die let them wit - ness his will

p *p* *cresc.*

A. In the blood - red mark revealed on my

fp *tr*

(Tears away

Più vivo.

A. breast: The Scar - let Let - ter —

cresc. e molto agitato

Più lento.
the ministerial band from before his breast, and sinks backward supported by Hester.)
A.
be_ _hold!
CORO.
Sopr.
Alto.
O wond_ _ _
Ten.
Basso.
O wond_ _ _
Più lento.
ff
er! Weird and aw_ful sign! Saw you the
er! Weird_ and aw_ful sign! Saw you the
Chill. (crouching in despair on the Pillory steps).
Thou hast es_caped me! Hadst thou sought the whole world
liv_ _ _ _ing tok_ _ _ _en bale_ _ful
liv_ _ _ _ing tok_ _ _ _en bale_ _ful
fp
fp

C.
ov - - er, no place or high or low - ly couldst thou have found where -

blaz - - ing, ov - er his heart tracing its fear - ful san - guine line?

blaz - - ing, ov - er his heart tracing its fear - ful san - guine line? —

p *fp*

C.
in — to baffle me whol - ly, — save this mean

p tr

Hester.

C.
scaf - fold's bound.

H.
O Arthur, look not far from

espress. *p* *dim.* *pp*

H.
me! Here — close am I, and my love — replies to the

cresc.

H.
light of thine eyes.
pp
H.
Turn thou not a_way! Ah, wither, then does thy spirit stray?
Arthur.
Ay, Far to wan_der we planned, Dear Hest - er,—
p
A.
thou and I— to a foreign strand.
pp

A.
But now I voy - age beyond the sky
A.
and the land I seek, the land of death!
p
Un poco più vivo.
Hester.
Wait, Arthur, wait! for dost thou not re - mem - ber,
p cresc.
H.
I told thee in the for - est thou
f

(Arthur sighs, looks at her longingly, then dies.)

H.
shalt not go a_lone?
Ha! Hast thou fled me,-
p
pp
cresc. e rit.
dim.
L.H.
so swift_ly gone?
My dearest one,-
(Takes out from her bosom the poison phiál.)
rit.
o soul__be_loved?
Thee,
a tempo
cresc.
Allegro.
then, I'll fol_low!
The poignant draught

21181

H.
brewed by our en - - e - my's fate - ful craft, will give me re -
H.
lease. Thou, too, dear Arth - - - - ur, didst
H.
from it seek free - - - - dom; and I sought to
H.
save thee. 'Twill save me from
p
mf espressivo
espressivo
f

H.
life: And sweet to my lips
p
H.
its cold - - - - - ness
H.
comes, as the
H.
cool winds that blow from

H.
mount - - - - - - - - - - - - - - - - - - ains
perdendosi
white for - ev - er with snow.
pp
Ped.
(She drinks the poison and dies.)
Thou shalt not go a - lone!
perdendosi
CORO
Ha!
Ha!
pp rit.
p

Andante, non troppo lento.

CORO I.

Sopr. *pp*
Hush! Hush! Hush!

Alto. *pp*
Hush! Hush! Hush! Hush!

Ten. *pp*
Hush! Hush! Hush! Hush!

Basso. *pp*
Hush! Hush! Hush! Hush!

CORO II.

Sopr. *pp*
Hush! Hush! Hush!

Alto. *pp*
Hush! Hush!

Ten. *pp*
Hush! Hush! Hush!

Basso. *pp*
Hush! Hush! Hush! Their souls are

Andante, non troppo lento.

24131

Their souls are fled.
Their souls are fled.
Their souls are
Their souls are fled.
Their souls are fled.
Their
Their souls are fled.
Their
Their souls are fled.
Their
fled.
Their souls are fled.
Their

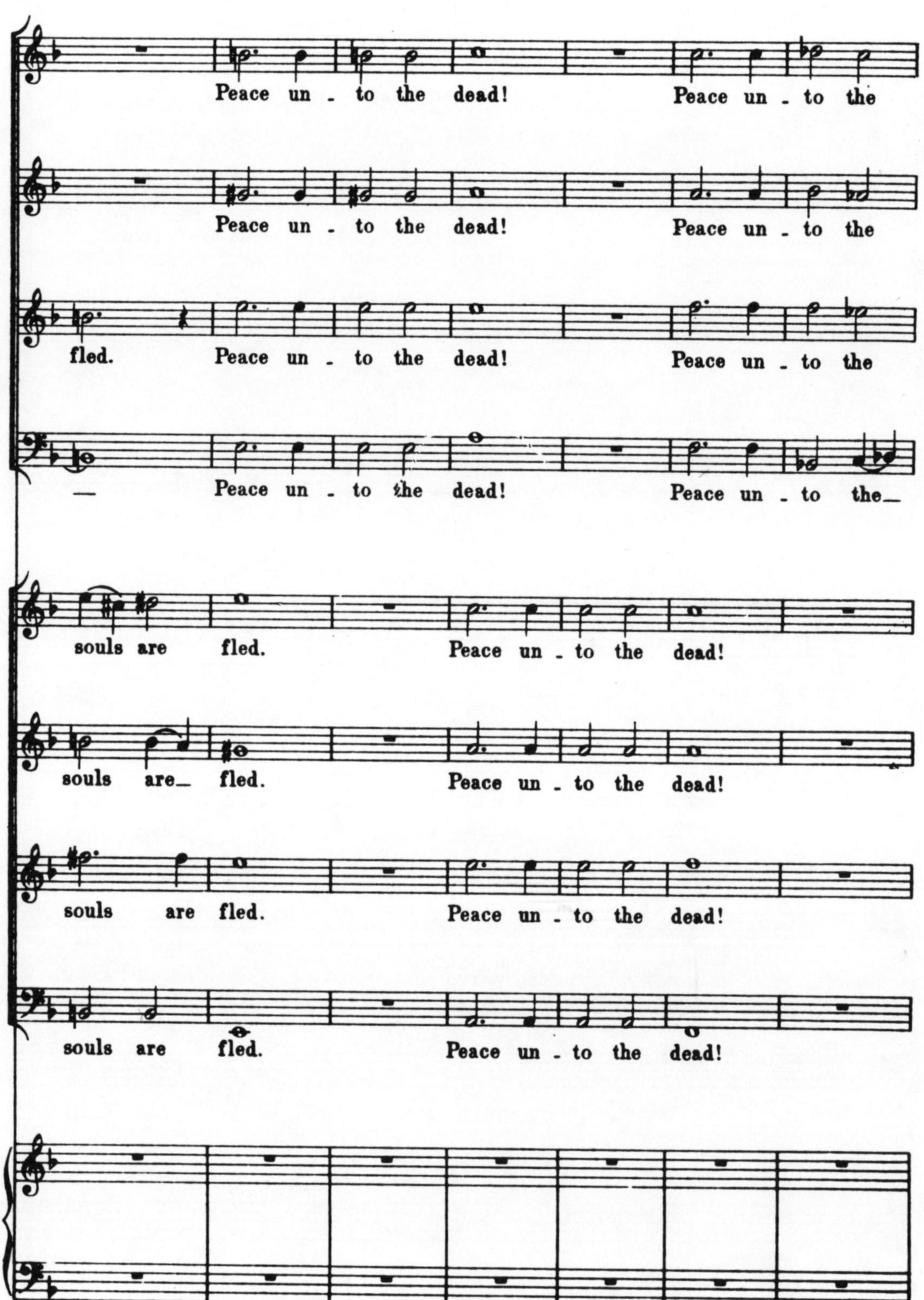
Peace un - to the dead! Peace un - to the
Peace un - to the dead! Peace un - to the
fled. Peace un - to the dead! Peace un - to the
— Peace un - to the dead! Peace un - to the—
souls are fled. Peace un - to the dead!
souls are— fled. Peace un - to the dead!
souls are fled. Peace un - to the dead!
souls are fled. Peace un - to the dead!

dead!
dead!
con espressione e
dead! The flow - er of
dead! The flow - - -
dim.
Peace un - to the dead, un - - to the dead!
dim.
Peace un - to the dead, un - - to the dead!
dim. con
Peace un - to the dead, un - - to the dead! The
dim.
Peace un - to the dead, un - - to the dead!

con espressione e sempre cresc.
The flow'r of sac-ri-fice blooms in no
con espressione e sempre cresc.
The flow-er of sac--ri-fice
sempre cresc.
sac-ri-fice blooms in no earth--ly
sempre cresc.
er of sac---ri-fice blooms
con espressione e sempre cresc.
The flow'r of sac-ri-fice blooms in no earth-ly
sempre cresc.
The flow-er of sac-ri-fice, the flow---er of
espressione e sempre cresc.
flow-er of sac-ri-fice blooms in no earth--ly
sempre cresc.
...blooms

earth_ly gard - en. Thou, Hest - er,
blooms in no earth - ly gard - en. Thou, Hest - er,
gard_en. Thou, Hest_er, o'er us
not on earth. Thou, Hest - er,
gard_en, the flow'r of sac - ri_fice blooms in no
sac - ri - fice blooms in no
gard_en, the flow'r of sac - ri_fice blooms in no
not on earth, blooms in no

o'er us tri - - - umph hast won; thou, Hest - er,
o'er us tri - - - umph hast won; thou, Hest - er,
tri - - - umph hast won; thou, Hest - er,
o'er us tri_umph hast won; thou, Hest - er,
earth - ly gard - en. Thou, Hest_er, tri - - umph hast
earth - ly garden. Thou, Hest_er, tri - - umph hast
earth - ly__ gard - en. Thou, Hest_er, tri - - umph hast
earth - ly gard - en. Thou, Hest_er, tri - - umph hast

dimin.
tri - - umph o'er us hast won, tri -
dimin.
tri - - - umph hast won, tri - - - - -
dimin.
tri - - - umph hast won, tri - - - - -
dimin.
tri - - - umph hast won, tri - - - - -
dimin.
won, tri - - - umph, tri - - - umph, tri - umph hast
dimin.
won, tri - - umph, triumph hast won, hast
dimin.
won, tri - - umph, tri - - umph hast
dimin.
won, tri - - umph, tri - - umph hast

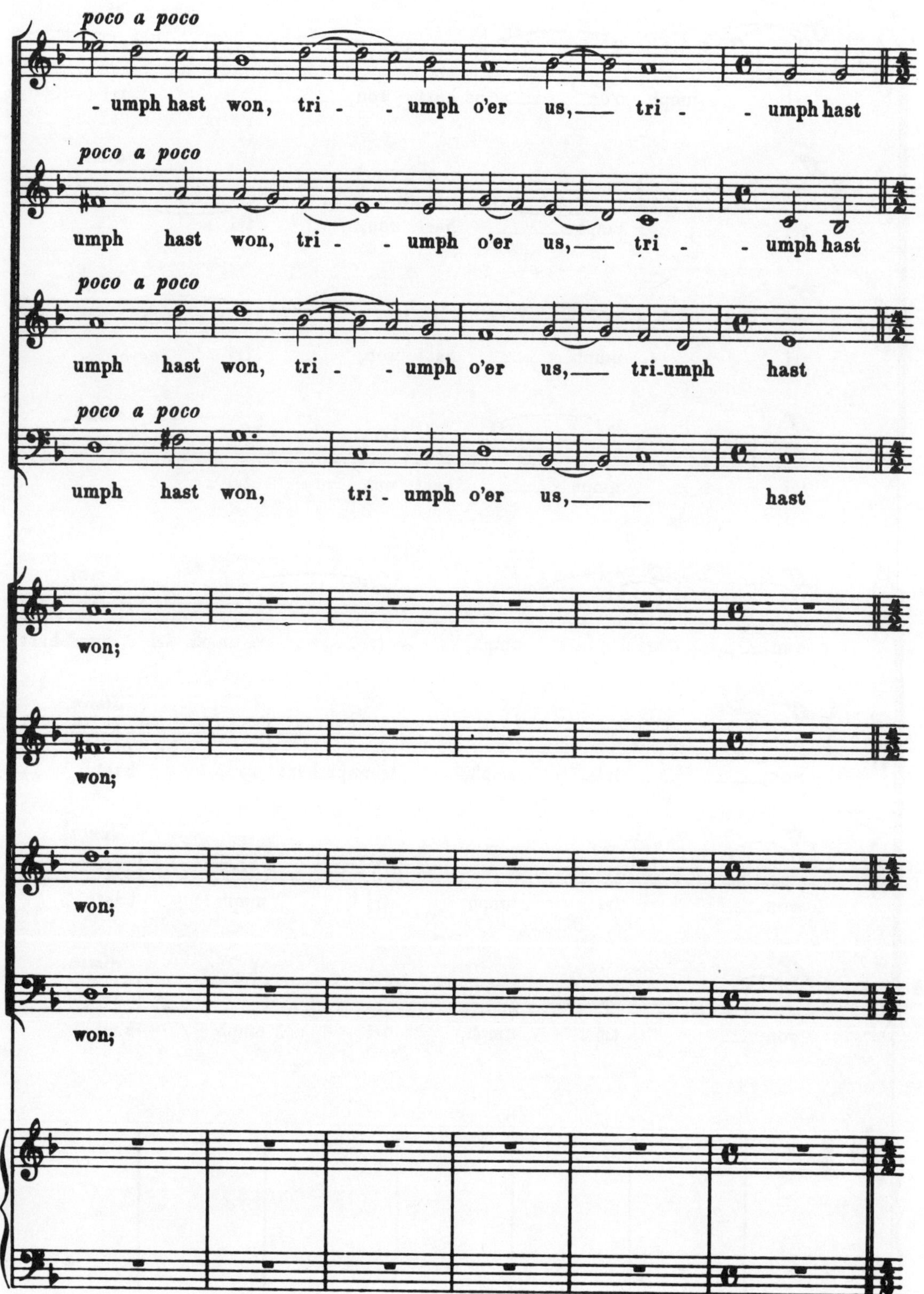
poco a poco
-umph hast won, tri - -umph o'er us,— tri - -umph hast
poco a poco
umph hast won, tri - -umph o'er us,— tri - -umph hast
poco a poco
umph hast won, tri - -umph o'er us,— tri-umph hast
poco a poco
umph hast won, tri - umph o'er us,— hast
won;
won;
won;
won;

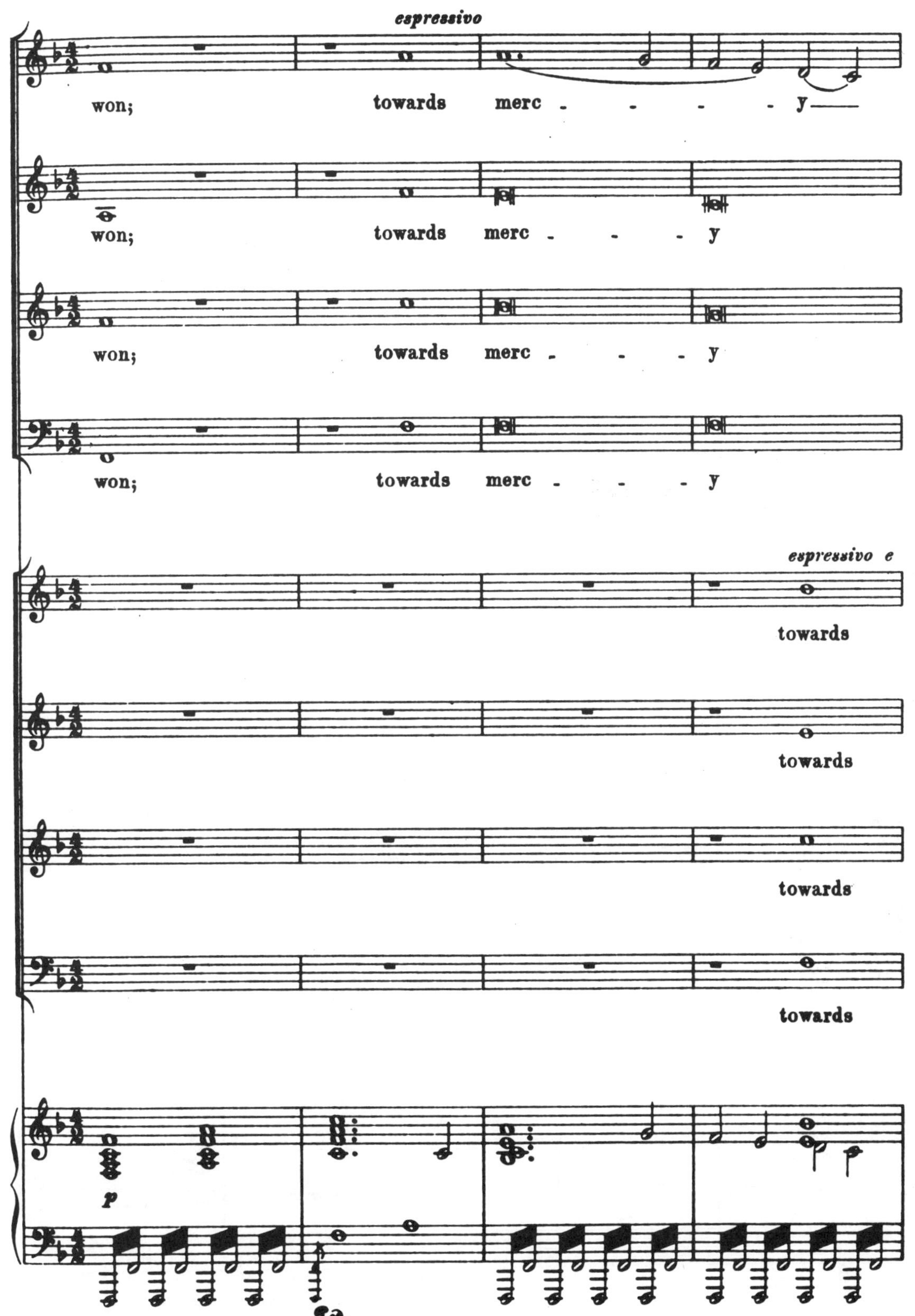
espressivo
won; towards merc - - - - y
won; towards merc - - - y
won; towards merc - - - y
won; towards merc - - - y
espressivo e
towards
towards
towards
towards
p
Ped.

21141

cresc.
turn - - ing our sul - len hate.
cresc.
turn - - ing sul - len hate.
cresc.
turn - - ing our sul - len hate.
cresc.
turn - - ing sul - len hate.
cresc.
merc - y turn - ing our sul - len hate.
cresc.
merc - - y our sul - len hate.
cresc.
merc - - y our sul - len hate.
cresc.
merc - - y our sul - len hate.
f
mf
Ped.

ff
Thou, Arthur, though re_pent_ing late,
ff
Thou, Arthur, though re_pent_ing late,
ff
Thou, Arthur, though re_pent_ing late,
ff
Thou, Arthur, though re_pent_ing late,
ff
Thou, Arthur,
ff
though re_pent_ing late,
ff
Thou, Arthur,
ff
though re_pent_ing late,
ff
Thou, Arthur,
ff
though re_pent_ing late,
ff
Thou, Arthur,
ff
though re_pent_ing late,
ff

may
may
may
may
may God thee pard - on!
may God thee pard - on!
may God thee pard - on!
may God thee pard - on!
dim.

God thee pard - on!
God thee pard - on!
God thee pard - on!
God thee pard - on!
Pard - on!
Pard - on!
Pard - on!
Pard - on!
espressivo
p
p
Ped.

Contents of the Series

Volume 1 British Opera in America
Children in the Wood (1795) and *Blue Beard* (1811)
Edited by Susan L. Porter

Volume 2 Early Melodrama in America
The Voice of Nature (1803)
Edited by Karl Kroeger
The Aethiop; or, The Child of the Desert (1813)
Edited by Victor Fell Yellin

Volume 3 Italian Opera in English
Cinderella (1831)
Edited by John Graziano

Volume 4 Later Melodrama in America
Monte Cristo (ca. 1883)
Edited by Anne Dhu McLucas

Volume 5 *Uncle Tom's Cabin* (1852) by George C. Howard and George L. Aiken
Edited by Thomas Riis

Volume 6 The Musical Stage Works of John Hill Hewitt
Edited by N. Lee Orr and Lynn Wood Bertrand

Volume 7 The Collected Works of Alfred B. Sedgwick
Edited by Michael Meckna

Volume 8	Pasticcio and Temperance Plays in America *Il Pesceballo* (1862) and *Ten Nights in a Bar-Room* (1890) Edited by Dale Cockrell
Volume 9	African American Theater *Out of Bondage* (1876) and *Peculiar Sam; or, The Underground Railroad* (1879) Edited by Eileen Southern
Volume 10	Irish American Theater *The Mulligan Guard Ball* (1879) and *Reilly and the 400* (1890) Edited by Katherine K. Preston
Volume 11	Yiddish Theater in America *David's Violin* (1897) and *Shloyme Gorgl* (189-) Edited by Mark Slobin
Volume 12	Early Operetta in America *The Doctor of Alcantara* (1879) Edited by Charlotte Kaufmann
Volume 13	Early Burlesque in America *Evangeline* (1877) Edited by Richard Jackson
Volume 14	Later Operetta in America, Part I *El Capitan* (1896) Edited by Paul E. Bierley
Volume 15	Later Operetta in America, Part II *The Highwayman* (1897) Edited by Orly Leah Krasner
Volume 16	Grand Opera in America *The Scarlet Letter* (1896) Edited by Elise K. Kirk